# Contents

1 WILLIAM ON THE TRAIL                                1

2 WILLIAM TAKES THE LEAD                             28

3 WILLIAM AMONG THE CHIMNEY-POTS                    60

4 WILLIAM'S THOUGHTFUL ACT                          88

5 WILLIAM'S TELEVISION SHOW                        109

6 WILLIAM DOES A BOB-A-JOB                         136

7 WILLIAM AND THE WEDDING ANNIVERSARY             157

8 WILLIAM AND THE NATIONAL HEALTH SERVICE         181

# An invitation from William

*Join my club and becum a n Outlaw*

*William Brown*

# You can join the Outlaws Club!
## You will receive
## ✳ a special Outlaws wallet containing
### your own Outlaws badge
### the Club Rules
### and
## a letter from William giving you the secret password

To join the Club send a letter with your name and address written in block capitals telling us you want to join the Outlaws, and a postal order for 45p, to

The Outlaws Club
Children's Marketing Department
18–21 Cavaye Place
London SW10 9PG

You must live in the United Kingdom or the Republic of Ireland in order to join.

# Chapter 1

# William on the Trail

'It's a public menace,' said Mr Brown.

'It certainly never seems to know which way it's going,' said Mrs Brown a little more mildly.

'Neither does Archie,' said Robert.

'It's fantastic,' said Ethel.

'I like it,' said William. 'It does more excitin' things than other people's cars.'

They were discussing Archie's new car. Archie Mannister was a feckless unpractical artist who lived at the other end of the village and who had recently astonished the neighbourhood by purchasing a second-hand car and taking driving lessons. Archie cherished a hopeless passion for Ethel and had been goaded to this desperate step by watching Ethel set off, Saturday after Saturday, in dashing-looking cars with dashing-looking escorts. Nothing, Archie realised, as he gazed despondently at the reflection of his thin vague face in the mirror, could make him dashing-looking, but at least he could buy a car. He bought the first car that was offered to him. It was an ancient, weary, disillusioned car, a car without spirit or enterprise or sense of adventure, a car that crawled docilely along the road, obeying clutch and brake and accelerator in a hang-dog, resigned fashion.

And by some miracle that no one had ever been able to explain Archie passed his driving test. Even Archie was puzzled by it. The only explanation he could offer was that it had been one of his 'good days' – one of the days when he remembered quite clearly which was the brake and which was the accelerator, when he reversed in easy masterly fashion without hitting anything. Archie did have those days but they were few and far between and it was a fortunate chance that one of them happened to coincide with the day of his driving test.

And then, quite suddenly, Archie saw his car as it really was. It was not, he decided, worthy of Ethel. It was not dashing. It was not modern. Beside the cars of his rivals it had a mouldering moth-eaten look. And then, by another unexpected stroke of luck, he sold a picture. It was a 'modern' picture, consisting of eyes, nose and mouth set at unusual angles in a face of unusual dimensions, the whole garnished, as it were, by a pair of compasses, a flight of building bricks and a bird of unknown breed perched on what appeared to be a newspaper rack.

An elderly widower who was contemplating marriage with a young lady of advanced artistic views saw the picture in the window of the shop in Hadley where Archie exposed his paintings for sale and went in and bought it.

'I'm not sure what it represents,' said the shopkeeper doubtfully. 'It may, of course, be symbolic, but I'm afraid I can't tell you what it symbolises.'

'That doesn't matter,' said the widower. 'She says she can't live with the "Monarch of the Glen" and it's about the same size, so it won't leave a mark on the wall-paper. They do if they aren't, you know.'

Archie had been dumbfounded to learn that his picture had been sold (he was not used to selling his pictures) and that the widower (who had made a good thing out of fish paste) had paid without protest the price that Archie had put on it. With a little adjusting of his finances he could now afford a new car, a real car, a dashing car, a car like the ones in which his rivals were wont to take Ethel out on summer evenings and Saturday afternoons.

The car that he bought was small, but it had zest and spirit and a sense of adventure developed to the highest degree. It was eminently dashing. It dashed continually and unpredictively. At a touch of Archie's foot on the accelerator it would dash up the nearest bank into the hedge. At a touch of his foot on the brake it would leap and buck like a spirited bronco. It was full of a lively and insatiable curiosity, investigating the contents of ditches and wayside ponds, experimenting with the middle of the road, the right-hand side of the road, the grass verge of the road and even the trees that bordered the road. It acquired a scratched and dented appearance but its spirit remained unbroken.

Ethel had been out in it three times. The first time it had run into a telegraph post. The second time it had turned in at Jenks' farmyard and come to rest on a midden heap. The third time it had entered a cul-de-sac and Archie, flustered and distracted, had been unable to reverse it, so he and Ethel had got out and walked home, leaving it there.

It was not only in the Brown household that Archie's car was being discussed, but Ethel's experiences lent, perhaps, a particular animation to the discussion, as the Browns sat drinking their after-lunch coffee.

'I've never yet known it end up at the place he'd set out for,' said Ethel.

'I hope you aren't letting him take you to the Jamesons' garden party in it this afternoon,' said Mrs Brown.

'You'll probably end up in the Hebrides, if you do,' said Robert.

'No, I'm not,' said Ethel. 'He can't get there till late, anyway. But I've promised to let him bring me home in it afterwards.'

'We'll take a long farewell of you, then,' said Robert.

'Well, I think Archie's is a jolly int'restin' car,' said William, 'an' it does some jolly int'restin' things, too.'

'Nobody asked you for your opinion,' said Ethel crushingly.

'And don't hang round listening to other people's conversation,' said Robert.

'Gosh!' said William indignantly. 'D'you think I *want* to? D'you think I've nothin' better to do than listenin' to you talkin' about Archie's car? D'you think I'm *int'rested* listenin' to you talkin' about Archie's car? Gosh! You mus' think I'm jolly hard up for things to be int'rested in if you think I'm int'rested listenin' to you talkin' about Archie's car. An' if—'

'Now, William,' interrupted Mrs Brown, 'it's a lovely afternoon. Go out and play.'

'Yes, I'm goin' to,' said William. 'I'm goin' with Ginger c'lectin' tadpoles in the pond an' let *me* tell *you* tadpoles are a jolly sight more int'restin' than listenin' to you talkin' about Archie's car an'—'

'*William!*' said Mr Brown sternly.

William went with silent dignity from the room, shedding both silence and dignity as he joined Ginger, who was waiting for him at the gate.

'Come on!' he yelled. 'I bet I catch more 'n' you an' I bet I get to the top of the fir tree an' I bet I get across the pond on that raft we made an' . . . Oh, come *on*!'

William and Ginger spent an enjoyable afternoon. They filled their jam jars with tadpoles. They climbed to the top of the fir tree. They got half-way across the pond in their improvised raft. They followed the course of the ditch beneath the road to where it came out on the other side. They tried walking on the wall of the pigsties in Jenks' farmyard and fell into the pigwash.

William's thoughts were fully occupied by these activities

and it was not till the end of the afternoon that they turned to Archie and Archie's car and the Jameson garden party.

'I'm goin' home by the Jamesons',' he said. 'I want to see Archie drivin' Ethel out of the gate. I like watching Archie drive out of gates. An' p'raps he'll give me a lift if I'm there.'

He reached the gate in good time. Archie and Ethel were seated in the car just setting off from the front door. A group of guests was assembled at the door to watch them.

'Good-bye,' called Archie blithely as he let in the clutch, pressed the accelerator and released the brake.

The little car gave a leap into the air, sprang across the drive into the shrubbery that bordered it and landed neatly in the middle of a Berberis Darwinii.

'Sorry,' called Archie. 'I'll reverse.'

He reversed, shot back up the drive, scattered the group of guests and charged with a dull grating sound into the wall of the house, detaching several strands of ivy.

'Sorry,' called Archie again. 'I think I'll manage it this time.'

But he didn't manage it that time. The little car seemed to have an unconquerable objection to the curved sweep of the drive that led to the gate. It leapt on to the lawn and broke down a couple of standard roses. It returned to the shrubbery to make sure of its victory over the Berberis Darwinii. It shot back into the drive again and tried to mount the steps to the front door. It returned to the lawn and laid low a bird bath and a garden table. It engaged in an unequal struggle with the gate-post, shot back yet again to the front door then returned undaunted for another round with the gate-post. Archie's face was pale and tense, his brow glistening with perspiration. Ethel's lovely mouth was set in lines of fury. The guests watched anxiously from behind the front door . . . till at long last the little car – its bonnet festooned by sprigs of Berberis

Darwinii, ivy trailing from its roof, half a standard rose dangling from one handle, and pieces of garden table adhering to wings and bumper – sailed jauntily out of the gate into the road.

And there William was waiting for it with his jam jar of tadpoles. Mud-stained stockings were rucked round mud-stained legs. His shirt was torn. His face – and indeed his whole person – bore marks of his passage through the ditch that ran beneath the road. Even his hair stood up in mud-encrusted spikes and the slime he had collected during his brief immersion in the pond added a greenish tinge to the whole. He was the last bitter drop in Ethel's cup of humiliation. William himself was unaware of anything unusual in his appearance.

'Hi, Archie!' he yelled. 'Will you give me a lift home?'

'Certainly,' said Archie, glad to be able to seem to stop the car, which had chosen this moment to stop of its own accord.

William clambered into the car, spilling a few tadpoles on the way, and settled himself happily in the back seat.

The car started again, and, its high spirits exhausted for the moment by its performance in the Jameson drive, proceeded decorously down the road.

Then Ethel's pent-up fury broke out.

'HI, ARCHIE!' YELLED
WILLIAM. 'WILL YOU
GIVE ME A LIFT HOME?'

'I've never seen such an exhibition in all my life,' she said.

'Exhibition?' said Archie. He was aware that the Jamesons' drive had presented certain difficulties, but he had surmounted them. He had – finally and triumphantly – driven out of the gate. 'I don't know what you mean.'

'I'll tell you what I mean, then,' said Ethel hysterically. 'I never thought I'd *live* to be made such a fool of as you've made of me. Backwards and forwards, backwards and forwards, till I was nearly *dead* with shame. I'll never forget it if I live to be a hundred. Look at us! We might be a travelling Harvest Festival with half the Jamesons' garden hanging on to us. If you think—' Archie changed gears and her voice could not be heard again till the echoes of his gear-changing had died away. 'Backwards and forwards till I was nearly seasick.'

'A certain amount of manoeuvring was necessary in the

circumstances,' said Archie, adding with a touch of pride, 'I
got into reverse quite successfully each time.'

'Got into reverse!' echoed Ethel, almost weeping with rage.
'I feel as if I'd been on one of those ghastly switchbacks in a
fair. And everyone I know watching me! I shall never be able
to look anyone in the face again.'

'I'm sorry you feel like this, Ethel,' said Archie with quiet
dignity. 'I did my best.'

'Well, this is the end,' said Ethel. 'I tell you here and now
this is the end.'

'What end?' said Archie, bringing the car from one side of
the road to the other with a swift deft turn of the steering-
wheel.

'The end of everything. I've finished with you. I don't
know why I ever started with you. I don't ever want to see
you again as long as I live. You're the most impossible creature I've ever come across in the whole course of my life. You
moon about, pretending to be an artist. You couldn't hold a
proper job for a week. I—I—I *despise* you.'

The worm did not often turn but quite suddenly it turned
now.

'I shall prove that you're wrong, Ethel,' said Archie distantly. 'I shall get a job and I shall keep it.'

'I'll believe that when I see it,' snapped Ethel.

They had reached the Browns' house now and Archie drew
up the little car at the gate with what was intended to be a
flourish but which turned out to be a complicated and highly
original ballet step. The suddenness of the finale detached a
strand of ivy from the roof and released several sprigs of
berberis.

'Here! Look out!' cried William. 'You're spilling my tadpoles.'

That brought Ethel's attention to his presence and afforded
her yet another grievance against Archie.

'And, to crown all,' she said, 'you've got to bring *that* object home in the car with us.'

'What object?' said William, mystified.

'You,' said Ethel tersely.

'Me?' said William, staring at her in honest bewilderment from his mud-encrusted countenance. 'What's wrong with me?'

But Ethel was already walking, head erect, blue eyes bright with anger, up to the Brown front door.

William scrambled out of the car.

''Fraid I've made a bit of a mess,' he said apologetically. 'I've spilt a bit of water an' tadpole an' some bits of mud seem to've come off from somewhere.'

Archie made no comment. He was staring in front of him, his thin face set and resolute.

Then, with a grinding of gears, scattering vegetation on all sides, the little car set off again down the road.

Ethel was known to be quick of speech and temper but quick also to forget what she had said in the heat of the moment, and the little incident might have been expected to end there. But it did not end there. Two days later the village was electrified by the news that Archie had applied for and obtained a job with a house agent in Fellminster, a small town just beyond Marleigh. It was not a very exalted job. It was, rumour had it, little more than an office boy's job, but Archie was evidently determined to do the thing in style. He discarded the corduroy slacks and colourful shirts that he had worn ever since he came to the village. He bought a city suit, a bowler hat, a rolled umbrella and an attaché case. He had been tempted to shave off his straggling reddish beard but his heart had failed him at the last moment and he had spared it.

Morning after morning the village would flock to its windows to watch Archie – in striped trousers, black coat and bowler hat, carrying the rolled umbrella in one hand and the attaché case in the other, an expression of dignified aloofness on his face – making his way to the station to catch the 8.15. Evening after evening the village returned to its windows to watch Archie – in striped trousers, black coat and bowler hat, carrying the rolled umbrella in one hand and the attaché case in the other – walking back to his cottage from the 5.25. The little car languished in the garage. The half-finished picture 'Sunset over the Mediterranean' languished on its easel. A week went by . . . two weeks went by . . . and Archie still made his daily journey to and from the station in stately dignity and city attire. The situation exasperated Ethel. It seemed to put her in the wrong and Ethel disliked being put in the wrong.

'Well, he's certainly holding the job,' said Mr Brown, impressed despite himself.

'The idiot!' snapped Ethel.

Meanwhile William and Ginger extracted what excitement they could from the passing hours. They made a space ship that took off from the roof of the tool shed in William's garden and landed on a bed of Mr Brown's treasured pelargonium cuttings. They got up a 'Zoo' in which William's dog Jumble (disguised as a lion) broke out of his cage and chased Ginger's cat Rameses (disguised as a mongoose) into the house, overturning a standard lamp and scattering a 'flower arrangement' that Ginger's mother had laboriously produced for a Women's Institute competition. They organised a floodlit racing track, fixing the floodlighting on the top of a rustic arbour by an ingenious paraffin device and provided an even more startling illumination than they had intended when the rustic arbour caught fire and the whole thing went up in flames. Then, having exhausted these pursuits, they turned their minds again to tadpoles.

'Let's make a tadpole pond in one of our gardens,' said William. 'Same as they make goldfish ponds. Tadpoles are a olly sight more int'restin' than goldfish, 'cause they turn into frogs an' goldfish jus' stay goldfish.'

'My fam'ly's sick of tadpoles,' said Ginger. 'They say I've got to bring another one near the place. My mother found one in the milk an' it made her mad.'

'Yes, mine's like that, too,' said William. 'I spilt some on the carpet with a bit of that green stuff I got off the pond for 'hem to eat an' she made an awful fuss.' He thought for a moment or two then said: '*Tell* you what! Let's make a tadpole pond in Archie's garden.'

'He'd stop us.'

'He can't. He's not there. He goes to that job in Fellminster every day now, you know, an' he doesn't get home till nearly six. He might stop us if he saw us doin' it but he won't. We'll have it finished by the time he comes home an' I bet he'll be jolly pleased when he sees what it looks like. An' it'll be jolly int'restin' for him to watch 'em turnin' into frogs. I bet he'll be grateful to us.'

They set to work at once, finding a battered tin bath on a refuse heap outside the village and mending the holes somewhat inadequately with chewing-gum.

'I bet it'll be all right,' said William hopefully. 'Chewing-gum lasts a jolly long time. I always swallow mine by mistake but if you don't it goes on lastin' on an' on an' on – for ever, prob'ly. We'll take it to Archie's garden an' dig a hole for it an' put it in an' fill it with water an' tadpoles an' it'll be a jolly nice surprise for him when he comes home.'

They took it to Archie's garden and set it down on the little lawn. William gazed at it critically.

'That chewin' gum doesn't look nat'ral,' he said at last. 'It'd look more nat'ral with stones at the bottom on top of the chewing-gum. I'll get some from that bed under the window.'

He went to the bed under the window, stood there for a few

moments, then returned to Ginger, an awestruck look on his face.

'I say, Ginger!' he whispered. 'There's someone in the house.'

'There can't be,' said Ginger. 'Archie's not come home yet.'

'Well, there is. Come an' listen.'

The two tiptoed across the lawn and stood by the window. There was no mistaking the stealthy furtive sounds that reached them from inside the cottage.

'Gosh, yes!' said Ginger.

'Let's go an' knock at the door,' suggested William, 'an' see if anyone comes.'

They went round to the front door. William beat a loud tattoo on the knocker. The sounds within the cottage ceased abruptly. A long silence followed. William beat another yet louder tattoo. They waited. No one came. There was no further sound or movement to be heard.

'Let's look through the windows,' said William.

But the windows only revealed the cottage in its usual state of confusion – the studio with its usual medley of canvases, palettes and paint brushes; the kitchen, knee-deep as usual in crockery, saucepans and household utensils; the sitting-room, chock-a-block with Archie's possessions, piled on table, chairs and writing-desk and overflowing on to the floor. They wandered round the cottage. The back door was locked, the windows fastened.

'It's jolly mysterious,' said William. 'It's like those stories in those books of Robert's.'

For William had recently whiled away a couple of wet days by browsing among Robert's collection of detective novels.

'Shall we go to the p'lice?' said Ginger.

'No,' said William. 'The p'lice aren't any good. They didn't solve a single crime in all those books of Robert's. Not a *single* one. An' it mightn't be an ordin'ry crime, too. Hardly any of those crimes in Robert's books were ordin'ry crimes. They seemed ordin'ry crimes to start with and then they got mixed up with international gangs an' secret treaties an' things and before you knew where you were they ended up with murder.'

'Gosh!' said Ginger.

'Yes, we've got to be jolly careful,' said William earnestly. 'You don't know what you're goin' to get mixed up in once you start. One of those books of Robert's seemed jus' an ordin'ry burglary in the first chapter – jus' an ordin'ry em'rald necklace – an' it ended up with half of them bein' blown up by dynamite an' the other half trapped in a burnin' ship.'

Ginger considered the situation in silence for a few moments.

'I think p'raps we'd better leave it to the p'lice, William,' he said at last.

'No, we jolly well *won't*,' said William. 'I bet I'm as good as any of those people that solved the crimes in Robert's books. They were all jus' ordin'ry people same as you an' me. In every single story I read I thought I could've done it as well as what they did. It's jolly lucky we've come across somethin' like this.'

'But what can we *do* about it?' said Ginger.

William looked at the cottage.

'Well, we've got to put the crim'nal off his guard to start with. We don't want him to think we suspect anythin'. We'll go away now jus' as if we didn't suspect anythin' an' we'll meet Archie's train an' come back with him an' find out what sort of burglary it was an' that'll be a sort of clue. It'll give us somethin' to work on.'

'All right,' agreed Ginger doubtfully.

Archie, emerging from the station in his faultless city attire, threw a frowning glance at the two boys who stood waiting for him.

'Well, what do you want?' he said testily.

It was plain that life as one of the world's workers had not improved Archie's temper.

'We jus' want to walk home with you, Archie,' said William, assuming a bland and innocent air.

Archie set off towards his cottage without replying. The two boys walked one on each side of him. William cleared his throat.

'I'm afraid we've got a bit of bad news for you, Archie,' he said.

Archie blenched.

'Ethel's not ill, is she?' he said.

'Oh, no,' William reassured him. 'She's jolly well. She was out with Ronald Bell in his car all yesterday so you needn't worry about *her*.'

Archie ground his teeth and gave a hollow groan.

'No,' continued William, 'the bit of bad news is that there's been a burglary at your cottage.'

'Nonsense!' said Archie. 'There isn't anything to burgle.'

'Well, you'd better go an' see,' said William. 'It mayn't *seem* a big burglary to you. It might be jus' an ordin'ry little thing like an em'rald necklace but it's what it's goin' to lead to that's serious.'

'Nonsense!' said Archie again. He opened the gate of his cottage and glared resentfully at the tin bath that lay in the middle of his lawn. 'Who's been throwing their rubbish into my garden?'

'It's your tadpole pond,' said William a little coldly. 'You'll be jolly pleased with it when we've finished it . . . I say, be careful goin' into the cottage, Archie. The crim'nal might still be there.'

Archie unlocked the door, flung it open and entered. A glance showed that the cottage was empty.

'Now will you boys please *go*!' he said.

'Jus' have a look at your valu'bles, Archie,' persisted William, 'jus' to see if anythin's missing.'

'I haven't *got* any valuables,' snapped Archie. 'At least, not to speak of.' He went into the kitchen, laid his bowler hat on the draining-board and glanced round the confused assortment of odds and ends that filled the room. 'There's the silver tea-pot my aunt gave me still on the shelf and' – he took down a jar marked 'sugar' and looked inside – 'my gold cuff-links are still here. I keep them here,' he explained with dignity, 'so that I'll know where they are. Those are my only valuables so there can't possibly have been a burglary and now' – with a sudden access of irritation – 'will you boys please go *away*!'

'Yes, we will,' said William. His face wore an expression of deep solemnity. 'Come on, Ginger.'

The two departed and began to walk slowly down the road.

'Well, nothin' was stolen so it's all right,' said Ginger.

'It's jolly well *not* all right,' said William. 'It's jus' the opp'site. That man we heard – well, I bet it was more than one. I bet it was a gang – wasn't out after valu'bles.'

'What was he out after, then?' said Ginger.

'He was out after' – William looked slightly self-conscious as he repeated the phrase he had come across in one of Robert's books – 'He was out after bigger game.'

'What bigger game?'

'P'litical,' said William. 'International secrets an' such like.'

'But Archie hasn't *got* any international secrets,' said Ginger.

'You never know,' said William. 'It's those that look as if they hadn't that have. Archie prob'ly isn't workin' at that house agent's place at all. He's prob'ly workin' at a secret place where they make secret atom bombs an' secret treaties an' things like that. I bet that's what this gang's after – not his aunt's tea-pot or his cuff-links . . . Anyway, we can find out.'

'How?' said Ginger.

'Easy,' said William. 'We'll go tomorrow afternoon an' see if they've come back. If they've come back it means that they're out after bigger game. They're still lookin' for somethin' an' what they're lookin' for's some secret papers that Archie's got. P'raps he doesn't know they're important. P'raps he doesn't even know he's got them. I bet he doesn't even know he's got them. He's the sort of person who wouldn't. One of the people in Robert's book didn't know he'd got them till the crim'nals kidnapped him ... We'd better go armed, 'cause they'll prob'ly be desperate. I'll take my water-pistol. You can practic'ly stun a person with a water-pistol.'

'An' I'll take my air gun,' said Ginger, his interest in the situation growing, 'then I can shoot 'em when you've got 'em stunned.'

They visited Archie's cottage the next afternoon with the same results as before. Approaching it cautiously, they heard the same stealthy furtive movements, which stopped abruptly when they sounded the knocker. No one answered the door and a prolonged inspection of the rooms through the windows revealed no signs of the intruders.

'Well, that *proves* it,' said William as they walked away. 'They've come back an' they're lookin' for the papers ... It's gettin' jolly serious, Ginger. We've got to put Archie on his guard. We'll meet him at the station same as we did yesterday an' we'll make him *see* that his doom's goin' to be sealed if we don't do something about it.'

'I bet he won't listen,' said Ginger. 'I bet he'll turn snappy the minute he sees us.'

Ginger was right. Archie turned snappy the minute he saw them.

Emerging from the station barrier with a straggle of other city workers, dejected-looking and sombre in his dark suit

'PLEASE GO AWAY AND LEAVE ME ALONE,' SAID ARCHIE.

and bowler hat, he frowned irritably as his eyes lit on the two
boys who stood waiting for him.

'What do you want *now*?' he said. 'I wish you wouldn't
hang about like this.'

'They've been again, Archie,' said William mysteriously.

'Who have?' said Archie, striding down the road so quickly
that it was all they could do to keep up with him.

'The gang,' said William. 'The one you're in the coils of.
The one that didn't steal your aunt's tea-pot 'cause they were
out after bigger game.'

'I don't know what you're talking about,' said Archie, 'and
will you please go home and leave me alone.'

'No, we'll stay with you, Archie,' said William reassuringly, 'an' I bet you'll be jolly glad we helped you before it's
finished. Your head's in the jaws of death an' you're goin' to
find it jolly difficult gettin' it out.'

Archie strode on without answering. The two followed him
up the little path to the front door and, ignoring Archie's gesture of dismissal, pressed forward into the cottage.

'Have any of your important papers been stolen, Archie?'
said William, looking anxiously round the little sitting-room.

'Papers about death rays or atom bombs or secret treaties,'
said Ginger.

'I do wish you'd stop talking nonsense,' said Archie queru-
lously, hanging his rolled umbrella from the chimney-piece.

'But, Archie, do look an' see if any of your important
papers have gone,' said William.

An expression of anxiety flashed over Archie's face. He
went to the drawer where he kept the few letters that Ethel
had written to him – an answer to an invitation to a cocktail
party, a letter of thanks for some flowers he had sent her on
her birthday, a reminder that his subscription to the tennis
club was overdue – then drew a breath of relief and closed the
drawer.

'Now, once again, will you two boys *go*!' he said. His eyes
went to the window and he added acidly, 'and take your tin
can with you.'

'I've told you that's your tadpole pond,' said William. 'We
started it but it didn't seem much use goin' on with it till we
know what's goin' to happen to you. We—'

But at that point Archie propelled them with an ungentle

hand on to the doorstep and closed the door behind them.

'Well!' said William indignantly. 'That's a nice way to treat a visitor.'

'P'raps he doesn't think of us as visitors,' said Ginger.

'Well, we're detectives, anyway,' said William, 'tryin' to solve his crime for him. Gosh! The people in those books of Robert's never shoved their detectives out of the house like that an' shut the door on them. He doesn't know how to *act* with detectives. I've a good mind to' – again a phrase from one of Robert's books occurred to him and he ended self-consciously – 'I've a good mind to throw up the case.'

'Yes, let's,' said Ginger. 'There's a new tractor at Jenks' farm. Let's go an' watch it working.'

'No,' said William. 'We can't leave Archie to his doom like that. He's up to his neck in this sea of crime an' we've got to help him. We've got to find out what this gang's after. It's not his aunt's tea-pot or his secret papers. 'Least, it may be his secret papers that they've not found yet. Anyway, we'll come back tomorrow an' find out some more about it. We'll be goin' into deadly danger but those detectives in those books of Robert's jus' didn't think anythin' of goin' into deadly danger. They walked into dens of crim'nals same as you or me'd walk into a sweet shop.'

'I think I'll make my will again,' said Ginger thoughtfully. 'I'll leave everything to my mother this time. There's not much use us leavin' things to each other if we're both goin' into this deadly danger together.'

'Yes, I'll do that, too,' said William. 'I'll leave my c'lection of insects to the British Museum same as I did before, but I'll leave all the other things to my mother.'

The next afternoon they approached the cottage with redoubled caution.

'We'll look in the windows first this time,' said William, 'an' see if we can catch 'em in the act.'

They crept on all fours up to the studio window and peeped into it from the shelter of a bush. William gave a gasp. For there in the room stood a man dressed in corduroy slacks and a vivid check shirt, a man with a thin harassed face and a straggling red beard – Archie's very self, as it seemed. William grabbed Ginger's arm and drew him away. Swiftly the two made their way back to the road.

'It was Archie!' gasped Ginger.

''Course it wasn't Archie,' said William. 'Archie's at that job in Fellminster. We saw him pass the

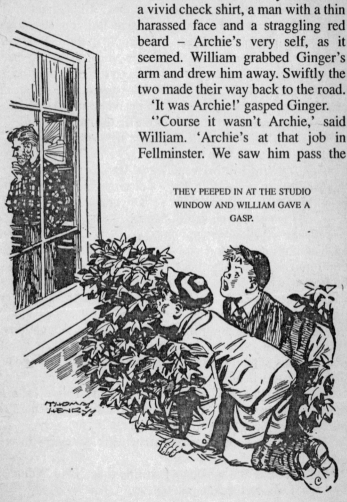

THEY PEEPED IN AT THE STUDIO
WINDOW AND WILLIAM GAVE A
GASP.

window this mornin' on his way to the station an' he doesn't get back till after five.'

'Who is it, then?' said Ginger.

'It's his double or his twin brother,' said William. 'It's all turnin' out a jolly sight more complicated than what I thought it was at first. There's a detective called Sherlock Holmes in one of those books of Robert's an' he said, "We're in deeper waters than I had thought, Watson." I'm goin' to be that one. He was jolly clever. You can be Watson. He jus' asked questions an' said: "Excellent, Holmes", an' things like that.'

'Well, I'm jolly well not goin' to be him, then,' said Ginger, who occasionally rebelled against William's leadership.

'You can make s'gestions same as he did,' conceded William, 'but they gen'rally turned out wrong.'

'I bet mine won't,' said Ginger. 'Anyway, Archie hasn't got a twin brother.'

'How d'you know he hasn't?'

'He'd have talked about it if he had.'

'He prob'ly doesn't know,' said William. 'He was prob'ly stolen away at birth. Gosh! We jolly well *are* in deep waters, Watson.'

'Well, what's he doin' in Archie's cottage?' said Ginger.

'That's what we've got to find out,' said William. 'Listen, I've got an idea. There's some money comin' to Archie that p'raps Archie doesn't know anythin' about an' this villain – he's either his twin brother or his double – is plottin' to murder Archie an' come into the money 'stead of him. It's prob'ly a gang. They'll put Archie out of the way, then this twin brother or double'll come into the money an' they'll share it out. We were jolly lucky to get away without him seein' us. He'd have murdered us straight off if he'd seen us. In all those books of Robert's they always murder the ones that know too much.'

'Gosh, it's gettin' a bit dangerous,' said Ginger, 'an' I don't see that there's anythin' we can do about it now.'

'Yes, there is,' said William. 'We've got to find out if Archie knows anythin' about this money that's comin' to him or this twin brother or double. We won't frighten him but we'll sort of put him on his guard. It's gettin' jolly near the chapter where the murders start, so we've got to be careful.'

'I bet Archie won't take any notice of us,' said Ginger.

And Ginger was right. Archie, emerging from the station barrier again, glared ferociously at the two boys who again stood waiting for him.

'I wish you boys wouldn't *haunt* me like this,' he said irritably. 'I'm tired after a day's work and I haven't the patience to put up with it. What do you want now?'

Again they took their places on either side of him and began to accompany him down the road.

'You know this money you're comin' into, Archie?' said William with an elaborate attempt at nonchalance.

'Don't talk such nonsense,' said Archie. 'I'm not coming into any money.'

William exchanged a meaning glance with Ginger.

They walked on for a few moments in silence, then William, in the same casual nonchalant fashion, remarked: 'You remember that twin brother of yours that was stolen away at birth, Archie?'

'I'm not going to answer any more of your ridiculous questions,' snapped Archie.

William exchanged another meaning glance with Ginger. Again the trio walked on for some moments in silence. Then William returned to the attack.

'Funny things, doubles, aren't they, Archie?' he said. 'I 'spect you've got one, haven't you?'

Archie ignored the question.

'I think you'd better be jolly careful about this double of yours, Archie,' continued William. 'He may *seem* all right but I bet he's diff'rent from what he seems. I bet he's after this

money that's comin' to you an' that you don't know anythin'
about an'—'

Archie turned on them like something at bay.

'Clear off, both of you!' he said, 'I'm sick and tired of
listening to your nonsense.'

They turned and walked slowly away. William shook his
head mournfully.

'You can see he's got somethin' on his mind,' he said, 'an'
I bet it's this double. I think it's a double, not a twin brother. I
bet Archie knows more about it than what he makes out he
does. Poor Archie! I bet he doesn't know which way to turn –
up to his neck in this sea of crime with his head in the jaws of
death.'

'Well, we jus' can't do more than we've done,' said Ginger,
who was beginning to tire of the situation. 'I don't see it's any
good goin' to his cottage again, anyway.'

But Archie's cottage held by now an irresistible fascination
for William.

'Yes, we'll go tomorrow,' he said, adding darkly, 'an' let's
hope we won't be too late.'

The next afternoon they approached the cottage more cautiously than ever, crawling from bush to bush and even making
their way on all fours over the sparse little lawn. No sound came
from within the cottage. Growing bolder, they looked in at
all the windows. Every room was empty of human occupancy.

'Gosh!' said William. 'I b'lieve we *are* too late.' He stiffened
suddenly. 'Listen! I can hear someone in the garage. Let's go
'n' see.'

They went to the ramshackle shed used by Archie as a
garage. The door was closed but, applying their ears to it, they
heard curious sounds – a wheezing sound, a strange grunting
sound.

'It's him,' whispered William. 'It's the double. I'm goin' to
lock the door an' capture him.'

A bar with a padlock hung across the door. William rammed it into place and closed the padlock. The sounds inside the garage continued.

'Well, we've got him captured,' said William. 'That's a jolly important thing to've done. Now let's go into the cottage an' see if we can find some clues.'

The cottage afforded an easy entrance. The back door stood invitingly open. They entered and went from

INSIDE THE CASE WAS ARCHIE'S CITY SUIT.

room to room. No one was there . . . but on the table in the studio lay Archie's attaché case.

'I'm goin' to open it,' said William. 'There might be a clue in it.'

He opened it and gave a gasp. Inside, neatly folded, was Archie's city suit.

'Gosh!' he said. 'That's a clue all right. This double's murdered Archie an' he's put this clue in here to drop in a river or somewhere. He prob'ly pulled the suit off him an' dragged him to the garage to murder him. I bet he was murderin' him in the garage when we heard those funny noises. Come on, Ginger! Quick! Let's go 'n' listen again.'

They ran to the garage and listened again. The garage was now as silent as the cottage.

'Yes, I'm afraid we're too late,' said William. 'Pity we locked the door, 'cause we've not got the key to unlock it . . . We've got to get help now, Ginger. We've got to get someone to unlock that shed an' find out what's happened. Come on!'

They ran out to the road. The road was empty except for Ethel, tripping lightly along on her way to the village.

'Come quick, Ethel!' panted William. 'Archie's been murdered.'

'*What?*' screamed Ethel.

'He's been murdered,' repeated William.

'He can't have been. He's in Fellminster.'

'He's not,' said William. 'He's in the garage.'

The three hastened to Archie's garage and stood looking at the padlocked door. No sounds came from within. It was Ethel who discovered the key hanging from a nail by the side of the shed. She unlocked the padlock and flung open the door. For a moment it seemed as if William's forebodings were justified. Archie reclined in the back of the car with his eyes shut. But at the sound of the opening door he started up and at the sight of Ethel his thin face radiated joy and surprise.

'Oh, *Ethel*!' he said.

'What on earth is all this, Archie?' said Ethel. 'I thought you were in Fellminster.'

'Oh, Ethel!' said Archie, scrambling out of the car. 'I'll make a clean breast of it. I've been longing to . . . I lost that job in Fellminster at the end of a week, but I was too proud to tell you and I went on going up to Fellminster in those awful clothes and I used to change into my ordinary clothes and a raincoat and a hat that came right down over my face in a sort of outhouse just outside Fellminster and I came back here by bus and through the woods and across the field and no one ever spotted me and I'd spend the day messing about here and then I'd go back by the same way, with my suit in my attaché case and change into it and come back by the 5.25. I was going to spend this afternoon seeing to the car and pumping up the tyres, but the pump leaked and I couldn't get any air in however hard I tried and I thought I'd have a bit of a rest, so I got into the back of the car and dozed off. I dreamed that I was taking you out in the car again and then I woke and found you here.'

Ethel burst into a peal of laughter.

'Archie, you are ridiculous . . . and I'm so glad about that stupid job.'

'Oh, Ethel, I've been so miserable and worried. I thought I'd lost you for ever.'

'Don't be so absurd, Archie,' laughed Ethel.

Ethel had missed Archie. Her other boy friends were attentive and correct, but she had missed Archie's dog-like devotion and general idiocy.

'Will you – will you let me take you out in the car again?' said Archie eagerly.

'Of course,' said Ethel.

She had missed Archie's car, too. She had missed its gaiety, its irresponsibility, its high spirits, its gallant disregard of danger. The cars of her other boy friends were large and handsome but lacking in imagination, their horizons bounded on all sides by the narrow limits of the Highway Code.

'Really, Ethel? . . . Oh, when?'

'There's no time like the present, is there? I'm here and the car's here and you're here.'

'Can Ginger an' me come too?' said William.

He was sorry not to have brought a desperate criminal to justice, but a ride in Archie's car would compensate for the disappointment.

Archie beamed at him, all his ill-humour gone.

'Certainly, boys. Certainly,' he said.

They scrambled into the back seat. Archie and Ethel took their seats in front.

The little car seemed glad to be released from confinement. It sprang out of the garage with an air of joyous abandon. It changed its mind and sprang back into the garage again, dived on to the lawn to inspect the tin bath, found its way by a miracle out of the gate; then, leaping, curvetting, bounding light-heartedly from side to side, it sped on its way down the road.

# Chapter 2

# William Takes the Lead

William raised a blackened face from the smoking fire.

'I think it's cooked,' he said. 'Come on. Let's eat it.'

The other Outlaws raised blackened faces and watched in happy anticipation as William withdrew the rusty saucepan from its nest of half-burnt twigs.

Inside the saucepan were the smoked remains of a couple of sardines, three sausages, a handful of patent cat food, a dollop of custard, four pickled walnuts, the scraping of a tin of golden syrup, half a bottle of sour milk, a soupçon of Gentleman's Relish, a dash of mouldy mint sauce, some cheese and bacon rinds and the tail end of a bottle of Henry's father's tonic – the whole blended and cooked by William. It formed a meal from which all four would have turned with loathing and disgust had it been offered them in their own homes, but they consumed it – sitting round the small clearing in the wood, eating in turn from the screw-top of an old honey jar that did service as a spoon – with undiluted pleasure.

'Well, it was jolly good,' said William at last, scraping a bit of burnt cat food from the bottom of the saucepan and putting it into his mouth. 'It was one of the best I've ever cooked.'

'There were some funny tastes in it,' said Henry reminiscently, 'but I liked them all.'

'I think it would have been better without your father's tonic,' said Douglas.

'It was jolly good tonic,' said Henry. 'The advertisement said it was, anyway. It said it would make a new man of him.'

'Well, did it?'

'He seemed the same to me,' said Henry.

'Let's try a bit of soda-water in the next lot,' said Ginger. 'My father's got a squirter an' I could easily pinch a bit.'

'A cipher,' said William. 'I know 'em. My father used to have one. I did a *smashing* squirt with it once, right from the sideboard out of the window and on to the rose bed. I didn't know my father was weedin' the rose bed an' he got it right in his ear. Gosh! He was mad.' He investigated the burnt fragments in the saucepan. 'Hi, Jumble! Here's a nice bit of cheese rind.'

But Jumble, who was worrying a stick on the outskirts of the group, merely cocked an ear, thumped his tail apologetically on the ground and continued to worry his stick. Jumble was a dog who was willing to try anything once. He had tried William's cooking once and found it enough.

'I suppose he's not hungry,' said William, putting the bit of cheese rind into his own mouth. 'Can't think why my mother makes such a fuss about cookin'. Seems easy enough to me. You jus' put things into a saucepan an' wait till they start smokin' an' then they're cooked.'

'The Chinese eat birds' nests,' said Henry with a modest air of erudition.

'That's a good idea,' said William with interest. 'I've never tried 'em but I bet they'd taste all right. We'll have one the nex' feast we do. It ought to mix all right with other things. Most things do.'

'French people eat snails,' said Ginger, who was sitting astride Douglas, pushing leaves down his neck.

'I tried a snail once,' said William. 'I didn't like the taste of it. I think it'd been dead too long.' He put the saucepan and screw-top into the hole in the tree that they occupied during the intervals between his 'feasts'. 'When I'm grown up I'm goin' to start a rest'rant an' I'm goin' to cook mixtures same as I do here an' people can eat 'em sittin' on the ground same as we do an' I bet everyone'll want to come to it. It's tables an' chairs an' knives an' forks that spoil ordinary grown-up meals. I bet I make my fortune an' when I've made it I'm going to—'

'Well, what'll we do *now*?' said Ginger, knowing that William, once launched on the subject of his future careers, was not easy to check.

William, brought back to reality, considered the question.

'Let' go 'n' see if we can find any of the Hubert Laneites,' he said at last. 'It's time we had another bash at 'em.'

During the past week the feud between the Outlaws and the Hubert Laneites, never dormant for long, had flared up and given a new zest and excitement to life. The two sides were, on the whole, pretty evenly matched, Hubert and his friends making up in cunning what they lacked in courage and strength. Yesterday morning Hubert had sent a syringeful of soapy water (put out by Mr Lane for use against the green-fly on his roses) full into William's face as he passed the gate, taking refuge behind a closed and bolted front door before William could rally his forces. Yesterday afternoon the Outlaws had met the Hubert Laneites in open warfare and put them to flight. The time was ripe for further hostilities.

Douglas rose to his feet, precipitating Ginger on to the ground. Even Jumble dropped his half-worried stick and set off joyfully with his friends in search of the Hubert Laneites, carrying his bushy tail like a banner to battle.

But an exhaustive search of the neighbourhood revealed no sign of Hubert or his followers. Their favourite haunts were empty and forsaken; the Lane house presented a closed front door and deserted garden.

It was as they neared William's house that the amazing sight

met their eyes . . . for there, issuing from the gate, they saw
Mrs Lane – massive in flowered silk dress and feathered hat –
and, by her side, the plump, smug figure of Hubert himself.

'Gosh!' said William aghast. 'She's been to tell my mother
about the bashin' we gave him yesterday.'

But the gracious smile that Mrs Lane bestowed on them as
she passed them made the explanation unlikely. And Hubert
himself smiled at them – a nauseating smile, oily, sly, full of
malicious triumph. The Outlaws turned and stood watching
the departing figures. Their mouths had dropped open in surprise, their brows were furrowed in perplexity.

'Go-sh! What are they after?' said Ginger. 'Goin' into your
house, William! What have they been to your house for?'

'I'll find out,' said William grimly. 'I'll soon find out.
P'r'aps the rest of you'd better go. My mother said you'd not
got to come here today, anyway, 'cause she didn't like us
usin' her new vegetable sieve prospectin' for gold yesterday . . . It mus' be about lunch time, so let's meet at Ginger's
after lunch an' I'll tell you all about it.'

'All right,' agreed the others.

They wandered down the road, casting puzzled glances
back at the Brown homestead, while William, mouth and
brow set in lines of stern resolution, entered the front door
and flung open the door of the sitting-room.

Robert and Ethel were on the settee, studying a small
account book. Mrs Brown was re-tying round her waist an
apron that she had evidently taken off in honour of her visitors. The expressions they turned on William reflected something of his own disapproval.

'*Must* you come *banging* into a room like that?' said Ethel.

'What's Hubert Lane an' his mother been here for?'
demanded William.

'William, your face is *black*,' said Mrs Brown. 'What *have*
you been doing?'

'Cookin',' said William shortly and repeated, 'What's Hubert Lane an' his mother been here for?'

'Your hair looks as if it had been dragged through a hedge backwards,' said Ethel.

'It has,' said William, casting his mind back over the events of the morning.

'And you've got part of a haystack sticking to your sleeve,' said Robert.

'It's not a haystack. It's a sardine bone,' said William, detaching it and putting it into his mouth. 'An' what I want to know is, what have Hubert Lane an' his mother been here for?'

There was a faint look of guilt on Robert's face as he replied,

'I suppose you may as well know now as later. The Hadley Dramatic Society is getting up a play and there's a small part in it for a boy.'

'Gosh! Why didn't you *tell* me?' said William. 'Well, there's no need for you to worry about *that*. I'll act it. Gosh! I could act *any* part. I'll act some of the other parts, too, if you'd like me to. Why, I've *wrote* plays. I've acted every kind of part there *is* in a play. I've been a ghost an' a pirate an' a Prime Minister an' a sword-swallower an' a murderer disguised as a detective an' – an' a leopard an' – an' a Voice of Doom . . . Why, in that play I wrote called 'The Bloody Hand' I acted *six* parts. I was a usurped king an' a deep-sea diver an'—' He looked at them helplessly. 'Why didn't you *tell* me about this part in this play?'

'I'll go and see to the lunch,' murmured Mrs Brown, thinking that Robert and Ethel could be left to deal with the approaching crisis.

'Why didn't you *tell* me?' repeated William as the door closed on her.

Actually Robert and Ethel – leading lights in the Hadley

Dramatic Society – had been at considerable pains to hide from William the fact that plans for a dramatic performance were afoot. William took a keen interest in every play that was produced in the neighbourhood and, when William took a keen interest in anything, strange developments were wont to follow.

'It's quite a small part,' said Robert, 'and it isn't a part that would appeal to you in any case. The play's about the Civil War and in the last scene this boy just comes in and says that he's seen the King's forces in flight towards Oxford. It's only one line.'

'Well, I could put more'n *that* into it,' said William.

'No, you couldn't,' said Robert.

'And he wears a velvet suit and a lace collar,' said Ethel with a note of triumph in her voice. 'You wouldn't want to wear that and you'd look awful in it, anyway.'

''Course I wouldn't want to wear it,' said William. 'But listen! I could wear a space suit. Ginger an' me are makin' a space suit. Listen! We'll have a space-boy comin' in a space suit an' bringin' a message from Mars an'—'

'Don't be ridiculous,' said Ethel. 'It's a play about the Civil War. You can't have "space" in a play about the Civil War.'

'I don't see why you can't,' said William. 'It wouldn't be so old-fashioned if you put a bit of space in it. Gosh! The Civil War's *jolly* old-fashioned. It was *years* ago. Why, it was before I was *born*. No one'd want to see an old-fashioned thing like that unless you put a bit of space into it to make it more modern. Listen! I'll be this space messenger an' I'll come in an' say that the flyin' saucers have come down an' you'll all put on your armour an' charge out to have a fight with these space men, an—'

'Do stop talking nonsense,' said Ethel. 'I tell you, you *can't* have a space episode in a play about the Civil War.'

'I'll be a Red Indian, then,' said William. 'Listen! I've got my Red Indian suit, so that'll save you the money you'd have spent on this lace thing. I'll come in an' say that the Red Indians have landed in England an' joined in the Civil War an' I'll bring in my braves – I'll be Chief Hawk Eye – an' we'll do a war dance and a war cry – I've got a smashing war cry – then charge out to fight the enemy . . . What d'you think of that?'

'Nothing,' said Robert.

'All right, if you don't want a Red Indian, I'll be an explorer,' said William. 'Listen! I'll be an explorer. I'll come back from climbin' a mountain where the foot of man's never trod. I'll bring in my sledge an' my husky – Jumble's a jolly good husky – an' I'll tell you all the things I've done . . . chasin' wolves an' buffaloes an' bein' chased by the 'bominable Snowman. No, listen! I'll *be* the 'bominable Snowman. That'd make it *jolly* excitin'. I'd come in dressed as the 'bominable Snowman. I could wear a sheet an' Ginger's got a *norful* mask that'd scare anyone out of their lives. I'll borrow that an' I bet *that*'d put a bit of excitement into this ole Civil War.' His smoke-begrimed face glowed with enthusiasm as another idea occurred to him. 'Listen! Let's have Ginger in it, too. An' Henry an' Douglas. They're all jolly good actors. An' I don't see why we need have this ole Civil War at all. If you'll let me make up a play for you, I'll make it a jolly sight more excitin' than any ole Civil War. Listen! We'll start with a space ship bein' hit by a meteor an' then we'll go on to—'

'Will-you-please-be-*quiet*!' said Robert, who had tried several times without success during the last few minutes to stem the tide of William's eloquence. 'You're not going to be in the play at all.'

William stared at him, open-mouthed.

'What?' he said.

'You're not going to be in it,' said Ethel, 'so that's that.'

'I thought you said there was a part in it for a boy.'

'There is.'

'*Gosh!*' said William as if unable to believe his ears. 'D'you mean you're goin' to act a play that's got a part in it for a boy and not let your own brother do it? Your own *brother*! Gosh, when I think of all the things I've done for you – postin' letters for you an' – an' going upstairs to fetch things for you an' – an' all the other things I've done – an' you won't do jus' a little thing like this for me. Your own *brother*! An' I'm a jolly good actor. I'd help you with this play. I keep tellin' you, I'd *help* you with this play. I've got hundreds of smashing ideas about plays an' there's lots of them I haven't tried yet 'cause no one would let me. I bet you'll be jolly sorry if you don't let me help you.' He gave his short sarcastic laugh. 'Well, if this play turns out all wrong with you not lettin' me help you, I hope you won't blame me, that's all.'

'No, we won't,' promised Ethel.

William was silent for a few moments.

'Listen,' he said at last with the air of one conceding a great favour. 'I'll do this boy's part same as it's wrote in the play. I'll jus' do a Civil War boy. I won't put anythin' of my own in it.'

'No,' said Robert.

'I won't put any space in or anythin'.'

'No,' said Ethel.

'I'll jus' do 'zactly what you tell me. I'll wear that lace suit.'

'No,' said Robert.

'I tell you I'll *help* you,' said William, his voice almost cracking with earnestness. 'I'll move the scenery about for you an' – an' work the footlights an' things like that.'

'*No*,' said Robert and Ethel simultaneously.

'GOSH YOU MUS' BE MAD,'
SAID WILLIAM.

'Well, if I don't do it,' said William, 'who's goin' to? That's what I want to know. Who's goin' to do it if I don't?'

There was a short silence. Obviously Robert and Ethel were reluctant to answer. Then Ethel summoned her courage and said with unconvincing nonchalance,

'Hubert Lane.'

William stared at her. His mouth had dropped open. His eyes were blank with horror. If his hair had not already been standing on end as the result of his morning's activities, it would have stood on end at this moment. Robert and Ethel averted their eyes guiltily from his accusing gaze.

'Who?' he asked hoarsely. '*Who?*'

'Hubert Lane,' said Robert.

'Gosh, you mus' be mad,' said William, flinging out his arms in an eloquent gesture. 'You mus' be *mad*, that's all. You couldn't not be mad to put Hubert Lane in a play an' not me. Gosh, you'd think anyone'd want their own brother in a play 'stead of Hubert Lane. Well, it's news to *me* if anyone wouldn't want their own brother in a play 'stead of Hubert Lane. Your own *brother*! Gosh, it's worse than Cain an' Abel. I jus' wouldn't have believed it if someone else'd told me. If someone else'd told me that you'd put Hubert Lane in a play an' not your own brother I jus' wouldn't have believed it. Gosh, when I think of all the things I've done for you . . . helpin' you clean your motor-bike an' faggin' tennis balls an' – an' all the other things I've done, an' then you put

Hubert Lane in a play 'stead of me. Hubert Lane? Gosh! Hubert *Lane*!'

'Now listen, William,' said Robert. There was a slightly propitiatory note in his voice; he could not but realise something of the insult he was offering William. 'As you know, I'm secretary of the Hadley Dramatic Society and it's badly in debt – so much so that, though we were considering this play, we didn't really know how we'd be able to carry it through. There's hardly any money for costumes and other things and I don't know who'd have lent us any . . . Well, Mrs Lane happened to hear about this play – that it had a part for a boy in it and that we were badly in debt – and she came along to offer to pay off half the debt on condition that we gave the part to Hubert. So you see the situation.'

'Well, listen!' said William. 'I'll pay off the debt if you'll give me the part. I've only got twopence-half-penny now, but I'll get some more. Jus' wait a bit. Wait till I'm grown up. I've got lots of plans to make me a millionaire when I'm grown up. I've got an invention for cleanin' chimneys that no one's let me try yet, but I bet it'll make my fortune.'

'Don't be idiotic,' snapped Ethel.

'We're sorry about it,' said Robert. 'We don't like Hubert Lane any more than you do, but needs must when the devil drives.'

'Gosh, yes, an' he *is* one, too,' said William bitterly. 'Anyway, I'll think out ways of gettin' this money. I—'

But Robert and Ethel

had vanished, fleeing before the threat of another deluge of
eloquence.

Lunch was a silent meal. William's appetite (that hardy
organ) did not fail him, but his expression was sombre, his
brow lowering, and he attacked his ample helpings of
shepherd's pie, stewed apples and custard with a ferocity
suggestive of one meting out punishment to his foes. His
family was relieved when, after his third helping of stewed
apples and custard, he made his dignified exit from the room.

The other Outlaws were awaiting him anxiously at
Ginger's house. There he gave an impassioned – if somewhat
incoherent – account of the situation.

'I'd challenge him to a duel,' he ended, 'but I've done that
before an' he never turned up. So I'm goin' to declare war on
him.'

'We're at war with him already,' Ginger reminded him.

'Yes,' but this is goin' to be a war of vengeance. A war
same as *savages*'d wage on someone that'd pinched their part
in a play.'

'War to the death,' said Henry.

Jumble barked eager agreement, jumping up and down,
waving his tail vigorously.

'I bet it lands us in a muddle,' said Douglas. 'An' we don't
know where he is, anyway. We couldn't find him this
mornin'.'

'I know where he's going,' said Henry. 'I was getting some
stamps for my mother at the Post Office an' Mrs Lane was
there an' she was sayin' that she'd got an aunt that'd never
been here before comin' over by the train that gets to Hadley
at three-fifty an' she couldn't go to meet her 'cause she'd got
to stay to go to a c'mittee meetin' an' Hubert couldn't meet
her 'cause he was goin' to play with his friends in the old
quarry so this aunt'd have to find her way to the house herself. So that's where he's goin'. He's goin' to the old quarry.'

'All right,' said William tersely. 'Come on.'

At the old quarry they took up their positions across the road and awaited the arrival of Hubert. And soon Hubert arrived, turning the bend in the road, accompanied by his gang. Hubert's gang was superior to William's in quantity if not in quality, for Hubert could always attach to himself a large number of boys of the baser sort by largesse of money and cream buns. They stopped short at sight of the Outlaws and stood irresolute, obviously meditating flight, but before they had time to collect their forces, they found themselves attacked in full force. Most of Hubert's gang melted away almost before the battle had begun, but Henry pursued Bertie Franks into the ditch, Douglas pursued Bertie's younger brother into the hedge, Ginger chased a thin ferret-faced boy called Eric Lorrimer up a tree and William got Hubert down in the middle of the road, sat astride his chest and, on a sudden inspiration, detached his Good Conduct Badge from the lapel of his coat and slipped it into his own pocket.

As quickly as they could the beaten remnants of Hubert's army disengaged themselves from their foes and fled to Hubert's home and safety. Drunk with victory, the Outlaws reeled back along the road towards their headquarters, the old barn.

'We got 'em licked,' shouted William.

In the excitement of the battle he had forgotten the little matter of the part in the play that had first roused his warlike spirit.

'I bet ole Eric's nose is bleedin',' said Ginger hopefully.

'We got 'em licked,' shouted William again, 'an' I've got his good conduct badge.'

Hubert treasured his good conduct badge. He won it with monotonous regularity. His form master disliked awarding it to him almost as much as Hubert enjoyed receiving it. Hubert's form master knew that Hubert was sly and mean and

WILLIAM DETACHED HUBERT'S GOOD CONDUCT BADGE
FROM HIS COAT LAPEL.

deceitful and as unpleasant a boy in general as you'd be likely
to come across in a month of Sundays, but Hubert was tidy,
Hubert was punctual, Hubert was unctuously polite and,
though Hubert's form master searched desperately each term
for some reason that would justify him in not giving the
badge to Hubert, he had never yet succeeded in finding one.
And Hubert paraded his good conduct badge. He wore it in
season and out of season. It was even rumoured that he slept
with it pinned on to the lapel of his pyjama jacket.

'I bet ole Hubert's mad,' chuckled William. 'I bet he's
*ragin'* mad. I bet he jus' doesn't know what to do without it. I

bet he can't walk or talk or eat or sleep without it. Gosh! Ole Hubert without his good conduct badge! Gosh! Ole—'

It was at this moment he noticed the absence of Jumble. He had last seen him in the thickest of the fray, leaping up and down, waving his plume-like tail uttering short sharp barks of excitement. Something of William's exuberance faded. He looked anxiously around.

'Where's Jumble?' he said.

They had reached the old barn now and they stood in the doorway scanning the landscape.

'He *was* there,' said Douglas vaguely.

''Course he was there,' said William, whose anxiety was increasing every moment. 'I've got eyes, haven't I? Gosh, he's my dog, isn't he? I ought to know when he's there an' when he isn't, oughtn't I? Well, it's news to *me* if I don't know when my own dog's there an' when he isn't. 'Course he was there. What I want to know is, where's he now?'

'He prob'ly gone off for a run on his own,' said Henry. 'He does sometimes.'

'Yes, he does,' said William, somewhat reassured. 'He's a jolly intelligent dog, is Jumble. He's gone off on his own to have a think. He thinks a lot, Jumble does. I've never *known* a dog think as much as Jumble. I bet he's a better thinker than most yumans. You'd be *s'prised* how much he thinks. Why, only yesterday—'

'Look! There's Bertie Franks,' interrupted Henry.

They stared at the approaching figure. Bertie Franks, Hubert's lieutenant – almost as plump and smug-looking as his chief – was slowly making his way to them across the field. He carried a white handkerchief on the end of a walking-stick.

'He's a truce,' said Ginger.

'A delegation,' said Henry.

'He's goin' to say somethin',' said Douglas more simply.

Bertie Franks had now reached the group and had fixed William with an oily, if slightly nervous smile.

'You've got to salute an' stand to attention,' said William sternly.

Had it not been for the smudges across cheek and brow and the strange angles at which his tousled hair stood out from his head, he would have been a highly impressive figure. Increasing the oiliness of his smile, Bertie Franks saluted and stood to attention. William returned the salute, raising a grubby hand to a grubby brow. Then,

'Speak, knave,' he said in a hoarse throaty voice, for William was apt to employ archaic phraseology to mark any moment of deep historic significance. 'An' if Hubert wants his good conduct badge back,' he went on in his ordinary voice, 'he can jolly well come an' get it. Tell him *that*. Tell him he can jolly well come an' get it.'

For answer Bertie Franks drew an envelope from his pocket, thrust it into William's hand then turned to flee back over the field as fast as his legs could carry him. The envelope was addressed to 'Mister William Brown Eskwire' and bore a red smudge in one corner that might have been a sinister sign of vengeance or, as Ginger hoped, an unpremeditated tribute from Eric Lorrimer's nose.

William drew out a sheet of paper and read:

'We've kapchered your dog as a hostidge. He'll be hung, drorn and kwortered if you don't send bak Hubert's good konduct bage by five o'clock.'

Hubert was an excellent speller but he had left the writing of the note to Bertie Franks, who was notoriously weak on that particular subject.

'Gosh!' said William, raising a horror-stricken face.

He looked around . . . There was no signs of Bertie Franks. With commendable wisdom, he had already made good his escape. It was clear what had happened. Jumble had valiantly pursued the retreating foe after the battle and thus delivered himself into their hands.

'Gosh!' said William again faintly.

His friends could only gaze blankly at him.

'You'll have to give him back the badge,' said Douglas at last.

'I jolly well won't, said William with a spark of his old spirit. 'I won't till I have to, till I'm drove by fate to. Five o'clock . . . *Anythin'* can happen before five o'clock. We'll try a rescue party first.'

'It won't be any good,' said Henry. 'They won't have put him anywhere where we can find him. They're too jolly cunnin'.'

'We'll try, anyway,' said William, his face pale with resolve. 'We'll jolly well try. An' if we don't find him I'll think out somethin'.' His unquenchable optimism was coming to his aid. 'I bet I'll think out *somethin'*. I've been in some pretty big jaws of danger before now an' I've gen'rally been able to think out *somethin'*.' He paused, frowned and drew a deep sigh. 'Gosh!' he said as his mind went over the events of the day. It seemed centuries since this morning when he had lightheartedly cooked his 'feast' over the smoking fire in the wood. 'Isn't it funny the way things go on *happenin'*? Seems sometimes as if they couldn't stop.' This philosophical reflection seemed to give him comfort. 'Come on. Let's start the rescue party.'

But Henry's gloomy forebodings were justified. No one answered their knock at the Lane front door. A cautious search of the Lane back premises and even of the old quarry revealed no signs of the missing Jumble. Disconsolately they returned to the old barn.

'Well, I thought you said you could think somethin' out,' said Ginger. 'You'll have to think jolly quick. There's not much time.'

William stared in front of him . . . and over his homely

grimy features a light slowly dawned. It was the familiar light that heralded one of his Ideas. The others watched him with respect tempered by apprehension.

'I've *got* it,' he said. 'It's a jolly good one, too. I bet it's one of the best ideas I've ever had. It's a *smashing* one.'

'What is it?' said Henry.

'Gosh, I *told* you,' said William. 'It's a smashing idea. It came quite sudden same as they do sometimes. My best ones always come sudden. They sort of spring out at me. I bet that's how ideas come to all great people like that man that saw a kettle boilin' over an' it set him off driving trains.'

'Yes, but what is it?' said Ginger, trying to bring William down to earth before he was carried away beyond recall, by the theme of his own cleverness.

'Well, listen,' said William. 'It's this.' He lowered his voice to a conspiratorial note. 'You know Henry heard Mrs Lane say that this ole aunt of theirs that'd never been to their house before was comin' to Hadley station by the three-fifty an' that she couldn't meet her an' neither could Hubert? Well, *we'll* meet her an' we'll pretend to be takin' her to Hubert's house an' we'll bring her here an' keep her for a hostage an' I bet Hubert'll have to come an' fetch her an' bring Jumble back. Gosh, it's a wizard plan. It couldn't go wrong.'

They stared at him, impressed, dimly aware that it *could* go wrong but unable for the moment to see how.

'It's not a bad one,' admitted Ginger.

'It's a smashin' one,' said William. 'Come on. Let's go'n' meet the train.'

Only one woman descended from the train at Hadley station. The four boys who stood in a row on the platform inspected her anxiously. But she was a reassuring sight – short and untidy, with mild eyes that peered from behind large dark-rimmed spectacles, a thin kind earnest face and unruly grey hair that had the appearance of having been blown about in a high wind. She looked wild and woolly and beautifully vague.

William stepped forward. He wore his most glassy-eyed wooden expression.

'We've come to meet you,' he said.

The lady smiled at them.

'What a charming idea!' she said.

'Hubert couldn't come,' said William.

'What a pity!' said the lady, 'but how kind of the rest of you to come! What's your name?'

'William.'

'Mine's Miss Taverton. And are these your friends?'

'Yes,' said William, 'they're my friends. We've come to take you to – well, to show you the way to it.'

'This is delightful,' said Miss Taverton. 'Quite delightful. Well, now let's set out, shall we?'

The little procession set out – Miss Taverton in front with William on one side and Ginger on the other, Douglas and Henry behind. The Outlaws were silent. Miss Taverton prattled brightly. She prattled about the weather and the countryside, commenting on the trees and flowers they passed, admiring a cow that gazed vacantly at them over a hedge.

'Such nice faces they have, I always think. Not intelligent, of course, but so kind and friendly.'

William had been afraid that she might have some idea of where the Lanes lived, but she raised no question or protest as they went through the village, still prattling gaily about the country sights and sounds.

'It's across this field,' said William as they reached the stile that led into the field where the old barn was. 'It's a sort of short cut to it.'

'Delightful,' said Miss Taverton, scrambling over the stile with unexpected agility. 'And which way do we go now?'

'This way,' said William, leading the way to the old barn.

Buoyantly their victim stepped over the threshold.

'Quite a roomy place,' she said, looking round.

William stood in the doorway, fixing her with his most ferocious scowl.

'You're kidnapped,' he said.

'You're a hostage,' said Henry.

'If he doesn't bring the other hostage back you'll be hung and drawn,' said Ginger.

'And quartered,' said Douglas.

'We're sorry about it,' said William, 'but our enemy's played a dastardly trick on us so we've got to play one back.'

'He's a villain of the deepest dye,' said Henry.

'An' it's no use tryin' to escape,' said William.

'Your doom'll be sealed if you try escapin',' said Henry.

'The whole place is s'rounded,' said Ginger. 'You can't see 'em 'cause they're hidden but they're jolly savage.'

'Gangsters,' said Douglas.

'Cut-throats,' said Henry.

'Fiends in yuman shape,' said William. 'They'd murder you soon as look at you if you tried to escape.'

'An' all the hedges an' ditches round are electrocuted,' said Ginger, 'so you'll be goin' into the jaws of death if you try gettin' out that way.'

'An' it's no good pleadin' for mercy,' said William, baring his teeth in a ferocious grimace, ''cause we've got hearts of stone same as all kidnappers.'

Their victim was not pleading for mercy. She was smiling at them in a pleasant, absent-minded fashion and investigating the interior of the old barn.

'She's tryin' to find a loophole of escape,' said William to Ginger, 'an' she jolly well won't find one.' He turned to his captive. 'Well, we're goin' now. We're leavin' this one' – he pointed at Douglas – 'to guard you. He's the most cut-throat of the lot' (Douglas smiled sheepishly) 'so you'd better not try gettin' past *him* . . . Come on.'

WILLIAM FIXED MISS TAVERTON WITH HIS MOST FEROCIOUS
SCOWL. 'YOU'RE KIDNAPPED,' HE SAID.

The three walked slowly across the field towards Hubert's house.

'Queer sort of aunt,' said William thoughtfully.

'Some of 'em are pretty queer,' said Ginger.

'I've got one that makes soup out of nettles,' said Henry.

'Well, we've got this one kidnapped all right, anyway,' said William. He took a grubby envelope from his pocket. 'I bet ole Hubert'll shake in his shoes when he reads this.'

Their minds dwelt with sombre satisfaction on the document enclosed in the grubby envelope.

'We've kidnapped your arnt for a hostidge. She'll be hung drorn and kwortered if you dont giv bak jumble at once.'

William uttered a sinister snort.

'Huh! I bet he'll bring old Jumble out quick as quick. If ole Jumble hasn't chewed him up first.' He chuckled. 'I say! That'd be a jolly good joke, wouldn't it, if ole Jumble's chewed him up. He's jolly cunnin', is ole Jumble. I shouldn't be surprised if he hadn't got taken prisoner on purpose jus' to get a chance to chew Hubert up.'

'Here we are,' said Ginger.

They stood for a moment or two at the Lane front gate; then, with grimly resolute expressions on their faces, walked up to the door and beat a tattoo on the knocker.

The door was opened by a tall stout woman with a beaked nose and majestic manner.

'Yes?' she said.

William stared at the stranger, a little nonplussed.

'Is Hubert in?' he said.

'No,' said the woman. 'Do you want him?'

'Yes,' said William.

'Are you friends of his?'

'No,' said William.

The woman looked nonplussed in her turn.

'Well, he's out and so is his mother. I'm his aunt.'

William's mouth dropped open.

'His—?'

'His aunt,' repeated the woman. 'I only arrived this after-noon. Actually I came by an earlier train than I'd meant to, but in any case both Hubert and his mother had engagements this afternoon. If you'd care to leave a message . . . '

William moistened his dry lips.

'No, 's all right,' he said hoarsely, crushing the envelope back into his pocket.

The woman gazed at him with dispassionate interest for a few moments, then closed the door.

The three walked slowly down to the gate.

'Gosh!' said William. 'His *aunt*. Who's the one we've got in the old barn, then?'

'I dunno,' said Ginger, adding with the air of one who has given deep thought to a weighty problem, 'Come to that, she might be anyone.'

'Gosh!' said William again. 'An' – an' there's ole Jumble . . . ' Anxiety for Jumble laid icy fingers on William's heart. Till now he had felt certain of countering Hubert's move and retrieving Jumble with honour and glory. But now . . . 'Gosh! If anythin' happens to old Jumble!'

'It never has yet,' said Ginger, though Ginger's heart, too, had sunk at this new turn of affairs. 'You've often thought he was lost an' he's always come back.'

'Yes, but he's never been kidnapped an' hostaged before,' said William. 'He's been nearly everything else – police dog an' husky an' St Bernard dog in the snow an' acrobat dog an' space dog but he's never been kidnapped an' hostaged before. He hasn't had any *trainin'* for it.'

'I bet Hubert doesn't know how to quarter anyone, any-how,' said Henry reassuringly. 'Or even draw 'em. I bet it takes a lot of practice.'

'Shouldn't be surprised if it isn't Jumble that does the quartering,' said Ginger.

'Yes,' agreed William, his volatile spirits rising again. 'I bet he makes ole Hubert sorry he ever started this drawin' an' quarterin' idea. Come on. Let's go an' have another look for him.'

'What about this woman that isn't Hubert's aunt?' said Henry. 'The one we've got imprisoned.'

'Oh, yes,' said William. 'Well, we left Douglas guardin' her, so—'

'Gosh! There's Douglas,' said Ginger.

Douglas was coming towards them down the road.

'Hi! What's happened to the prisoner?' said William.

'I thought I heard Jumble barking, so I went to look,' said Douglas, 'but it wasn't Jumble. It was that brown dog at the farm. Then I thought I'd come an' see how you were gettin'

'THIS DELIGHTFUL STRAY DOG HAS JOINED ME,' SAID
MISS TAVERTON. 'HE'S SHARING MY LUNCH.'

on. Hubert's aunt'll be all right. I bet we scared her with all those things we said to her.'

'Well, she's not Hubert's aunt,' said William, 'so we can let her go.'

'I bet she's gone already,' said Ginger.

'Well, we'll go 'n' see an' then we'll jolly well find ole Jumble an' rescue him,' said William. 'Come on! Let's hurry. It mus' be gettin' on for five.'

They ran back across the field to the old barn. And there an amazing sight met their eyes. Miss Taverton, looking wilder and woollier than ever, was seated on the ground eating sandwiches out of a paper bag, and, seated by her side, sharing the sandwiches, was a black and white mongrel from whose collar trailed a piece of broken rope.

'Jumble!' yelled William.

'This delightful stray dog has joined me,' said Miss Taverton. 'He's sharing my lunch. I meant to eat it on the train but quite forgot about it.'

Jumble was leaping up at William, greeting him exuberantly.

'Good ole boy!' said William with an unconvincing attempt at nonchalance. '*Good* ole boy!'

'He's your dog, is he?' said Miss Taverton with mild interest.

'Yes, he's my dog,' said William, his whole face shining with pride despite his efforts to appear unmoved.

'He's a nice fellow.'

'Oh, yes,' said William in as casual a voice as he could summon. 'Oh, yes, he's—'

'*Look!*' shouted Ginger. 'The Hubert Laneites!'

They turned and looked across the field. And there they saw the Hubert Laneites making their way furtively along the road, examining the ditches and hedges on either side. Hubert whistled beneath his breath. Bertie Franks called 'Hi, boy!' in a nauseatingly persuasive voice. It was clear that they were searching for their missing hostage.

'Come on!' said William shortly. 'Let's *show* 'em.'

'They've got sticks,' said Ginger.

'Where's our sticks, then?' said William.

Lying about the old barn were the sticks that the Outlaws had salvaged at various times from hedges or the woods – stout business-like sticks which they used as alpenstocks or jumping poles, as weapons of offence or defence, or merely for investigating ditches, fishing in streams or stirring up muddy ponds.

Their war cry rose in fierce challenge as they charged down the field. Again the battle was short and sharp. A crescendo of yells, a scrimmage of sticks ... and the Hubert Laneites turned in headlong flight to the safety of Hubert's home. Jumble came rollicking back with the victors, barking his triumph, waving his plume-like tail, dragging his broken rope as if it were a trophy of battle.

The Outlaws slackened pace as they saw their hostage standing at the door of the old barn, watching them with her pleasant dreamy smile.

'We've got to get rid of *her*,' said William. 'We don't want her stayin' in the old barn for the rest of her life same as she seems like doin'.'

'How'll we get rid of her?' said Ginger.

'I'll get rid of her,' said William shortly.

He approached Miss Taverton with an air of resolution.

'Well, you'd better be getting back now, hadn't you?' he said.

She turned her benign smile on him.

'Back where, dear?'

'Back where you came from,' said William. 'Well, you want to go back there, don't you? They're prob'ly expecting you back there where you came from. We'll take you to the station. There's lots of trains goin' from the station. You're sure to find one goin' back to where you came from.'

'That's very kind of you,' said Miss Taverton. 'Yes, perhaps it's time I made a move. It's all been so interesting. I've had a most enjoyable time.'

William gaped at her, bereft, strangely for him, of the power of speech.

The procession wended its way down the hill and towards the village. Jumble, his rope removed, was at the head of it. William and Miss Taverton followed. Ginger, Henry and Douglas straggled behind.

The confused events of the day were sorting themselves out in William's mind, bringing a vague sense of depression. He'd rescued Jumble, he'd beaten the Hubert Laneites, but still Hubert Lane was to take the part in Robert's play. Despite the stress and strain, the battle and the turmoil, he was back where he'd started.

They were passing William's house now and William's expression grew strained and a little nervous as he noticed Robert approaching from the opposite direction. He was aware that his wild and woolly companion would arouse his family's curiosity, and William avoided, as far as possible, arousing his family's curiosity.

'Let's get on quick to the station,' he urged. 'You don't want to miss that train goin' back to where you came from.'

'Oh, but I can't go before I've done the piece of business I came about, you know,' said Miss Taverton. 'That would never do. I'm afraid I've lost the letter with the particulars in it, but perhaps this gentleman could help me.' To William's horror she was approaching Robert. 'Excuse me, but could you tell me where the secretary of the local Dramatic Society lives?'

'Here,' said Robert indicating the Browns' front gate and adding simply, 'I'm him.'

'Well, may I have a word with you,' said Miss Taverton, 'if you could spare the time?'

'Certainly,' said Robert, throwing a harassed and bewildered glance at her companions. 'Come in.'

He ushered her up the path and in at the front door. The Outlaws held a hasty consultation by the gate.

'I told you we were goin' to get in a muddle,' said Douglas. 'I jus' don't know what's happenin'.'

'Neither do I,' said William helplessly. 'It's gettin' complicateder an' complicateder . . . '

'She's crackers,' said Henry. 'I bet she's escaped from somewhere.'

'Yes,' agreed Ginger, 'an' she's likely as not to turn dangerous any minute. They've got the strength of ten men, have lunatics.' He gazed with gloomy relish at the closed front door. 'I bet she's finished Robert off by now an' started on the others.'

'Crumbs!' said William. 'I'd better go an' see . . . An' the rest of you'd better go home. No use all of us goin' into the jaws of danger. Anyway, I don't suppose my mother's forgot about that vegetable sieve yet. I'll come round afterwards an' tell you what's happened.'

They stood watching him in fascinated horror as he vanished inside the front door, followed by Jumble.

Inside the sitting-room were Mrs Brown, Robert and Miss Taverton. The faces of Mrs Brown and Robert wore expressions of blank bewilderment. Miss Taverton's face wore its usual expression of vague benignity. She had flashed a woolly smile at William on his entrance.

'You were expecting me, of course?' she was saying to Robert.

'Well – er—' began Robert, but she went on without waiting for him to finish.

'I think I put the situation quite clearly in my letter. I can't remember whether I did or not because my memory is a little uncertain. I mean, so often I *think* I've remembered things and then find out that really I've forgotten them. But I'll go over the whole situation again to make it quite clear in case there was any ambiguity . . . You see, this friend of mine from America was very much impressed by some plays she saw performed by children at certain schools in England and wanted to do what she could to encourage the art of acting among English children. So, when she went back to America – she's a wealthy woman – she left me this sum of money to use at my own discretion to further the art of acting among English children. A sort of international gesture if you understand what I mean.

'Well, as you know, I put a tentative advertisement in a newspaper and you answered it.' Robert opened his mouth to protest, but she waved aside the protest before he could make it. 'You said that you had a flourishing little troupe of child actors and I agreed to come over and see them. I wrote and

told you the time I should arrive.' Again Robert's mouth
opened and shut silently as she plunged on with her recital.
'So you can imagine my pleasure when I found four of your
little troupe of child actors at the station to meet me. You had
told me in your letter that they hoped to make a children's
theatre in a sort of outhouse in the village and they took me
straight to it – it was a sort of barn in a field – and there they
acted a most delightful little sketch for me, making me the
chief character, which I thought a most *original* idea. I was
the kidnapped and they the kidnappers. I don't know which of
them had written it but they all remembered their lines and
spoke them with great expression and spirit.

'Then they left me alone for a time to prepare their next
little "turn" and I made a thorough inspection of the place. I
don't think it's *really* suitable for a theatre. It isn't weather-
proof and I don't think it could be made so. Such a pity!
While I was inspecting it a delightful stray dog joined me.'
She threw a vague smile at Jumble who was sitting at her feet,
looking up at her, following her recital, as it seemed, with rapt
interest. 'There he is! The dear fellow! He shared my lunch,
which I'd forgotten to eat on the train, and then the children
returned – the whole troupe this time – to do their second and
last little performance for me. They acted a tournament on
imaginary horses with sticks for lances. One side came up to
the barn and the other stayed in the road and then they
charged each other and held the tournament. It was a really
splendid piece of acting on the part of the little men.

'This little man' – she beamed fondly at William – 'simply
surpassed himself and he'd been excellent in the kidnapping
scene. I've had a most interesting and enjoyable day and' –
she turned an earnest gaze on Robert – 'I do congratulate you
on the junior section of your dramatic society. You must have
worked hard indeed to train them to such a fine pitch of per-
fection.'

There was a short silence, but Robert was too dazed to take advantage of it. He stared at her dumbly.

'So I really think,' went on Miss Taverton, 'that I couldn't do better than use my friend's gift to encourage the work you are doing here among these little people.' She turned to Mrs Brown. 'This is your mother, I think you said? You know' – she gave a deprecating little laugh – 'I've got such a hopeless memory that I've forgotten your name. I'd forgotten your address too, so it was a good thing I ran into your son so providentially at the gate . . . Actually, I'm afraid I've lost the letter you sent me. I could have sworn that I put it in my bag, but I've been hunting for it ever since and can't find it.' She opened her bag, plunged her hand into it and gave a little laugh of triumph. 'Ah, here it is! It had slipped through a hole in the lining.' She took out a letter and examined it. 'Rushton-Smythe! Of *course* that's your name!' She turned again to Mrs Brown. 'Now Mrs Rushton-Smythe—'

'My name's Brown,' said Mrs Brown faintly.

Miss Taverton gazed at her.

'Are you sure?' she said.

'Yes,' said Mrs Brown.

'But your son signs his name "Rushton-Smythe".'

'No,' said Robert. 'Mine's Brown, too.'

'How odd of you to sign your letter "Marmaduke Rushton-Smythe", then! Perhaps it's a sort of pen name.'

'No,' said Robert. He appeared to be fighting his way slowly and painfully through swirling mists of stupefaction. 'I never signed . . . I never . . . ' He looked at the letter that she held in her hand. 'I never wrote that letter.'

'How *very* odd!' said Miss Taverton. 'I can't understand it. You wrote a letter to me and signed it "Marmaduke Rushton-Smythe" and now you say you're called Brown and never wrote it.'

'Excuse me,' said Robert, taking the letter from her hand.

He studied it for a moment. 'I'm afraid you've come to the wrong place. You've come to Hadley and the letter was written from Hedley. Right up in the north.'

'Oh, dear!' said Miss Taverton with a rueful smile. 'What a foolish mistake! I simply haven't the brain of a flea.'

'Oh, I'm sure you have,' said Mrs Brown, politely reassuring.

'So you aren't getting up a children's play, after all?'

'No,' said Robert. 'We are getting up a play, but there's only one part for a boy in it.'

'And this fine little actor will be playing the part, I take it?' said Miss Taverton, waving a hand in William's direction.

William, finding himself under discussion, assumed his wooden glassy-eyed expression again.

'Well, no,' said Robert.

'Indeed? And who will be playing it, then?'

'A boy called Hubert Lane.'

'Now which was that? I remember hearing some of the names. It *wasn't* the fat one, was it?'

'Well, yes,' said Robert.

'Oh, *not* that one!' said Miss Taverton, clasping her hands earnestly. 'He was such a poor actor. He put no expression or spirit into his part at all. No, no, *this* little man must have it.' Again her hand waved vaguely in William's direction. 'He was *splendid* both in the kidnapping scene and in the tournament.'

'Well, you see,' began Robert and, summoning his scattered forces, gave her a brief summary of the situation.

'Oh, but I'm sure that can be adjusted,' said Miss Taverton. 'I'm sure that my friend would wish me to extricate you from your difficulties in order to give this little man his chance. He has real talent, you know, and real talent is so rare. My friend left the matter entirely to my discretion. I'll give you a cheque that will set you on your feet if this little man can have the part . . . I can get into touch later with these other people who live at – Hedbury, isn't it?'

'Hedley.'

'Oh, yes . . . and see what can be done about them, but I must put you on your feet first for this little man's sake.'

Bewilderment again submerged Robert. He struggled out of it as best he could.

'Well – er – yes that's very kind of you.'

He looked round for William, but William had vanished.

'Let me make you a cup of tea,' said Mrs Brown, feeling that, after a cup of tea, the whole situation might seem less fantastic.

'How very kind of you!' said Miss Taverton. She, too, looked round for William. 'And where's our little man? Ah, his heart is too full for words. He has gone to be alone with his emotion. A shy and retiring nature, like all true artists.'

William was upstairs in his bedroom, stretched out on his stomach on the carpet (his favourite position for creative work) busily writing with a blunt pencil in a tattered exercise book. Jumble lay beside him, wearing Hubert's good conduct badge on his collar, as a pledge and token that the Hubert Laneites feud was still at its height, and occasionally thumping his tail on the ground in encouragement.

William was re-writing his part in Robert's play – making it that of spaceman, detective, Red Indian, explorer, kidnapper and victor in a thousand tournaments.

# Chapter 3

# William Among the Chimney-pots

It wasn't often that William approved of Robert's girl friends, but he approved of Rowena.

Rowena and her father had recently come to live in Ilfracombe Terrace – a row of much-gabled Victorian houses on the outskirts of Marleigh – and Robert had lost no time in scraping acquaintance with her. Rowena was young and glamorous, and Robert was an expert at scraping acquaintance with the young and glamorous. As secretary of the Tennis Club, he could call to ask them to join the Tennis Club; as secretary of the Amateur Dramatic Society, he could call to ask them to join the Amateur Dramatic Society; as owner of a highly temperamental motor cycle, he could stage a breakdown at the beloved's gate and ask to use her telephone to ring up the garage. Failing all these, he could assume the expression of a traveller lost in the wilds and call at her house to ask his way, or, should she own a dog, smile on it benignly and profess a passionate interest in its breed.

Robert was no Don Juan. He was earnest and simple-minded, and each specimen of youthful glamour for which he fell was to him the One Great Love of his Life. Roxana Lytton had been the last One Great Love of his Life, but Roxana had become engaged to an air pilot with a handle-bar moustache (as soon as Robert saw the handle-bar moustache, he had known it would be fatal to him) and the post was temporarily vacant.

Actually very little finesse was needed to scrape acquaintance with Rowena. Robert met her at a party in Marleigh, saw her home, asked her to tea on the next Sunday and made 'dates' for a cinema on the following Saturday and a Young Conservatives' dance at the end of the month. Though earnest and simple-minded, Robert was a quick worker.

When she came to tea on Sunday, William had been prepared to treat her with the aloofness and contempt with which he usually treated the One Great Loves of Robert's Life. But there was no doubt that Rowena was different. She played with Jumble, throwing his rubber bone for him and working him up into an ecstasy of delight. She talked to William and showed an intelligent interest in his plans for making a lagoon from the stream in the wood, building a cable railway up the sides of the old quarry, with a rope, a pulley, and a wooden box, and organising a circus with Jumble as the star turn.

This did not, of course, commend itself to Robert, but the beloved generally had some weakness, and William was a weakness that could easily be dealt with. Robert dealt with him by the simple method of taking him by the collar and throwing him out of the room.

'Go and play with your scruffy little friends,' he said as he shut the door on him.

William didn't go to play with his scruffy little friends. He liked Rowena and thought he would stay on the premises to see how the affair progressed.

He went to the bottom of the garden and occupied himself by climbing on the roof of the tool shed and 'gliding' from it to the ground below.

But he was hovering in the background when Robert accompanied Rowena to the gate and took his farewell of her. He heard Rowena say: 'I wish I could ask you to tea, Robert.

I'll try to get round Daddy, but he's very difficult. He's terribly sweet but terribly difficult. You see, he hates people – especially young men.'

Robert watched her out of sight, his lips curved into a fond smile, which vanished abruptly when he turned to confront William.

'What are you hanging about for?' he said irritably. 'Good Lord! What a sight you look!'

William's gliding exploits had landed him – more often than not – in a heap of potting soil, prepared by Mr Brown, that lay at the foot of the shed, and his person bore ample traces of it.

'What's wrong with me?' said William indignantly, smoothing back his hair with both hands and sending a shower of potting soil down his neck. 'I look all right. I look same as I always do. I—'

'You look revolting,' said Robert. 'Thank Heaven Rowena didn't see you!'

WILLIAM HOVERED IN THE BACKGROUND WHILE ROBERT TOOK HIS FAREWELL OF ROWENA.

'I bet she wouldn't have minded,' said William. 'I bet—'

But Robert cut him short by an impatient snort and went indoors to the sitting-room, where Mrs Brown was ensconced in an arm-chair, darning his football jersey.

'Isn't she marvellous, Mother?' said Robert.

'She's very nice,' said Mrs Brown. 'You know, dear, you

really *will* have to get a new one. It's just held together by darns.'

'Nice!' echoed Robert. 'What a word! She's *marvellous*! And I wouldn't be seen dead in a new one.' He eyed the faded, washed-out, much darned garment affectionately. 'Good Heavens! No one has new football jerseys. It just isn't done.' The fond smile returned to his lips. 'Hasn't she got a wonderful smile?'

'I can't get the right red for the red stripes,' said Mrs Brown. 'It makes it look so odd.'

'I like it odd,' said Robert. He heaved a deep sigh. 'It's her father who's the difficulty.'

'Oh, yes . . . Professor Mayfield. He writes books on some obscure subject, doesn't he?'

'Economics,' said Robert reverently. 'But Rowena says he writes other books under another name.'

'What sort of books . . . ? Robert, *look* at this hole!'

'Just pull it together anyway,' said Robert carelessly. 'As long as there are enough threads to make it stay on me, that's all that matters. I don't know what sort of other books. Rowena says he keeps it a dead secret. She says he enjoys writing these other books far more than his books on economics, but he's ashamed of writing them so he doesn't let anyone know about them.'

'Improper love stories, probably,' said Mrs Brown placidly. 'Some of the modern ones are simply shocking. I can't think how printers can bring themselves to print them.'

'They may be, of course,' said Robert. 'It's a nice thought. But he seems an odd kind of man altogether. He's sweet to Rowena, but he hates people. He can't bear them. He won't let her ask anyone to the house. Miss Burnham, who lives next door, has tried hard to be neighbourly and so has little Mr Lupton, who lives next door to Miss Burnham, but he won't have anything to do with them. Miss Burnham's got a friend staying with her who's crazy to meet him because she once saw his name in a newspaper, and he just said "No, thank you" when she asked him to tea.'

'How very strange!' said Mrs Brown. 'The black stripes are easier, of course, but even so new black looks quite a different black from old black.'

'It makes it difficult for Rowena . . . It makes it difficult for me, too. I mean, when one likes a girl, one does like to be invited to her home. I mean, it *means* something to be invited to her home. I mean, it means that – well, it *means* something.'

'I'm sure she likes you, dear,' said Mrs Brown, as she drew out a strand of new red darning wool and laid it doubtfully against a discoloured gaping stripe of Robert's jersey.

Robert's tense expression relaxed again into the fond smile.

'Do you really think she likes me, Mother?' he said.

'Yes, dear, of course,' said Mrs Brown. 'I can't think why they have them in stripes. It would be much simpler if they were all one colour.'

Robert's smile had clouded over.

'Of course, there's Oswald . . .'

'Oswald?'

'Oswald Franks.' Robert gave a bitter laugh. 'You'd think with all the other girls there are in the world he could leave just one alone, wouldn't you? But – oh, no! He's got to fix on Rowena. Taking her out in his car, buying her chocolates and ridiculous armfuls of flowers. It's – it's ludicrous. He was summoned for obstruction only last month, too. You wouldn't have thought she would want to be seen about with a – a common criminal like that.'

'P'r'aps she wants to be a common crim'nal too,' said William. 'I saw a film about a girl crim'nal once an' she was jolly nice. She had a jolly intelligent dog, too. It smelt the house was on fire an' pushed her out of a window.'

William had intended to remain silent during the conversation so as not to attract notice to himself, but it was beyond William's power to remain silent during any conversation.

Mrs Brown turned her attention from Robert's football jersey to her younger son.

'William!' she gasped. 'You look dreadful. What *have* you been doing?'

'Me?' said William, opening his eyes wide. 'Nothin'. I've jus' been havin' a nice quiet game by myself in the garden.'

'You're filthy. And *look* at your stockings. Right down over your shoes. Where are your garters?'

'Garters . . .' said William blankly. 'Garters . . .' His mind went back over the day to a game he had played with Ginger in the morning. Ginger had been a gangster and William a policeman. William had captured him, and the garters had figured in the scene as handcuffs. He didn't know what had happened to them after that.

'Garters . . .' he said again, the blankness of his expression now verging on imbecility. 'Garters . . . did I have garters on?'

'Oh *course* you did, William,' said Mrs Brown. 'You had them on when you went out after breakfast. You looked perfectly neat and tidy.'

'That surpasses belief,' put in Robert.

'Where are your garters, William?' said Mrs Brown.

William knit his brows and assumed an expression of deep thought.

'Garters . . .' he said again meditatively. 'I'm tryin' to think what I did this mornin'. I do diff'rent things diff'rent mornings. What day is it today?'

'William, what's—happened—to—your—garters?'

'They may've worn out,' said William with the air of one who wrestles with an almost insoluble problem and edging towards the door as he spoke. 'Things do wear out . . . They may've worn out suddenly an' fell into pieces an' jus' dropped off ... or some thief may've taken them off me when I wasn't lookin'. A sort of cat burglar, p'r'aps, that wanted them for himself. He may've drugged me while he did it. He—'

'*William!*'

''Scuse me,' said William politely as he sidled through the doorway. 'I've jus' got to go an' see to somethin'.'

'Well, that's got rid of *him*,' said Robert. 'I forgot he was there. I only hope he doesn't go sticking his nose into my affairs. I wish Rowena hadn't been so nice to the little blighter. Once he gets interested in anything ...'

William was certainly interested ... And the rivalry between Robert and Oswald – a rivalry that had existed since their boyhood – stirred all his sense of family loyalty. Moreover, the affair didn't stop at Robert and Oswald. For Oswald's young brother, Bertie, was one of William's greatest enemies, a member of the gang with which William and his followers had waged unceasing warfare ever since any of them could remember. The situation was full of possibilities and he turned his whole attention to it.

He hung round the tall Victorian house where Professor Mayfield lived, he watched the stocky bearded figure of the professor as he sallied forth on his daily 'constitutional', he heard Miss Burnham and Mr Lupton greet him in pleasant neighbourly fashion, to be rewarded by an absent-minded grunt. And he watched the rivalry between Robert and Oswald gather force and venom.

Oswald had considerable advantages. He was polished and slick. He had a man of the world poise that was, on first acquaintance, very impressive. And he was the son of doting parents who supplied him with a handsome income in return for putting in an occasional appearance at his father's office. His boxes of chocolates were larger and flashier than

Robert's, his flowers more exotic; beside his car, blazing with yellow paint and chromium, Robert's motor cycle looked the cheap and nasty affair it was. But the sun of Rowena's favours shone equally on both of them. The smile with which she received Robert's offerings was fully as sweet as the smile with which she received Oswald's. She bestowed her slender form on the pillion of Robert's motor bike as readily and gracefully as on the rubber-filled, yellow-upholstered seat of Oswald's car. And a glint of mischief in her blue eyes showed that the situation was not without its appeal to her.

A similar situation, of course, had arisen some time ago, when Robert and Jameson Jameson had been rivals for the favour of a saucer-eyed beauty called Emmeline, and William and Victor – Jameson's younger brother – had loyally if mistakenly given what assistance they could; but Jameson was Robert's friend and Victor was William's and there had been a geniality about the affair that was lacking now. Jameson was, in any case, out of the running in this contest, for he was spending a harassed fortnight in charge of a scouts' camp some twenty miles away.

Gradually the whole thing boiled down to the question as to which of them would first win an invitation from the professor. There was something awe-inspriring in the large, shaggy figure – for the professor's beard was unkempt and he wore a long-haired overcoat that had grown patchy and dishevelled with the years – as it strode down the lanes on its daily constitutional. Its very gait discouraged friendly advances. But doggedly, unremittingly, the rivals continued their campaign. Had the professor been an observant man, he would have noticed two youths mutely dancing attendance on him at intervals throughout the day – opening his gate for him with smiles of obsequious politeness or removing obstacles from his path as he took his solitary rambles; but the professor was not an observant man and remained unaware of their existence.

Bertie, of course, played his part in the little drama. Bertie was mean and sly and cunning and he devised a series of unpleasant little tricks – placing drawing-pins, business-end up, on William's desk at school, stretching a string across the gateway to William's house as William returned to it at dusk. But William was not a boy on whom unpleasant little tricks could be played with impunity, and a personal encounter between the two brought Bertie to the reluctant conclusion that the unpleasant little tricks had better be discontinued. So he contented himself by jeering at William from the safe refuge of his own garden.

'Gosh, what a mingy little box of chocolates Robert took her! Crumbs! You should've seen Oswald's.'

'I say, William! Where did Robert get those flowers he took her yesterday? Out of the dust-bin, I shouldn't wonder.'

Bertie had a crude and limited sense of humour.

But his most successful manoeuvre was to rouse William's fear and anxiety by such remarks as:

'I say, William, Oswald's goin' to tea there tomorrow. What d'you think of that?' or 'William, the ole professor's asked Oswald to dinner tonight. Snooks for ole Robert!'

Though all of these statements turned out to be false, William never failed to feel a pang of horror and dismay as he heard the words.

And so things dragged on till the affair of the house painting.

'Daddy's going to paint the outside of the house,' said Rowena to Robert one afternoon as they returned from a visit to a Hadley cinema.

'*What?*' said Robert incredulously.

'Oh, yes, he loves house-painting,' said Rowena. 'He always paints the outside of our houses. He finds it a mental tonic. Like gardening, only he says that flowers get on his nerves and paint doesn't. Anyway, there it is. He's borrowing a ladder from Clements', the builders. He's going to start tomorrow.'

'Good Lord!' said Robert. 'It's incredible.'

But the next morning proved it true. A ladder was placed against the tall Victorian house, and the bulky figure of the professor, girt with a large white apron, could be seen moving to and fro with unexpected agility and applying paint to the woodwork with unexpected skill.

Again, had the professor been an observant man, he might have noticed the same two youths hovering below him, putting out tentative hands to steady his ladder, waiting with eager expectation for him to drop something ... but he remained still unaware of their existence. At the gate he might have noticed – but didn't – two small boys watching proceedings with tense interest and occasionally indulging in hostile assaults on each other.

'I bet he drops that paint brush in a minute an' I bet Oswald picks it up for him.'

'I bet he doesn't. I bet Robert does.'

'He nearly asked Oswald to tea yesterday ... Well, he *did* ask him to tea.'

'He didn't.'

'He did. He said Robert was a soppy fool. He said you were all soppy fools.'

William rose to the defence of his family, and the two vanished into the ditch. When they emerged to take up their stand again at the gate, Bertie's face was plastered with mud and William's tie stuck up at a curious angle at the back of his head.

Robert and Oswald turned round, their features contracted into an identical expression of fury.

'Go away!' they said fiercely between their teeth.

Though bitterly at variance on general grounds, they were at one in a constant fear of being made ridiculous by the activities of their younger brothers.

It was at the end of the week that Rowena sprang another piece of news on them.

'Daddy's got sciatica and the doctor says he must go to bed for a week.'

'Bad luck!' said Robert.

'I'm terribly sorry,' said Oswald. 'If there's anything I can do . . .'

The three were returning from the golf course on which Robert and Oswald had run a neck-to-neck race in 'showing off' to the beloved. Robert was the better player but Oswald had a more spectacular style.

'There's nothing anyone can do,' said Rowena. 'What worries him, of course, is the house. He'd done it all but one of the upstairs windows and the skylight on the roof, and Clements' have only lent him the ladder for a week. Still, it can't be helped.'

Robert's and Oswald's eyes met in a quick furtive glance. Their two minds had but a single thought, and each suspected that the other had it, too. Then casually, nonchalantly, as if to conceal the thought, Oswald began to talk about the weather and Robert to discuss the chances of the local football team in its next match.

But Robert was a transparent, ingenuous youth, and the clouds of worry still hung on his brow when he reached home.

'What's the matter now, dear?' said Mrs Brown, smiling at him in mingled exasperation, amusement, and tenderness, as she poured out his tea. Secretly Mrs Brown found her whole family exasperating, amusing, and a little childish.

Robert told her what was the matter now.

'You see, if only one could go along and finish it at once, the old chap would probably be so grateful that – well, everything would be plain sailing after that. And no one could deny that I'm a pretty good hand at painting.'

'Y-yes,' agreed Mrs Brown.

'If it weren't for Oswald . . . You see, he's planning to do it too.'

'Did he say so?'

'No, but I saw it in his eye. We can't do it this evening because of the party at the Bartons'. We're all going to it – Rowena and Oswald and me. But tomorrow morning' – his thoughtfulness turned to gloom – 'he'll be at it first thing. He'll spend the whole morning on it.'

'And why can't you?' said Mrs Brown.

'Because I've promised to go over and give Jameson a hand with his camp. I shall have to start with the dawn.'

'Couldn't you get out of it?' said Mrs Brown.

She knew, of course, that the whole thing was ridiculous; but her motherly pride in Robert could not endure the thought of his being worsted by the obnoxious Oswald.

'No, I can't let him down. He's counting on me. He's short-handed as it is. It's – it's extraordinary how fate seems to *dog* me. Things like this just don't happen to other people.'

William, who had so far managed to restrain his natural garrulity, now made his voice heard through a mouthful of bread and jam.

'Gosh! I've heard of worse things happenin' to people. I once read a tale about a man that was hangin' over the edge of a prec'pice bein' pecked at by eagles an'—'

Robert turned on him savagely.

'Shut *up*.'

'And don't talk with your mouth full, dear,' said Mrs Brown in mechanical reproof.

William finished his bread and jam, consumed a couple of raspberry buns in four large mouthfuls, then went down to the tool shed at the bottom of the garden with a view to perfecting his gliding technique.

It was just as he landed neatly in the middle of the heap of potting soil that the Great Idea came to him. For a moment he sat there motionless gazing into space, overwhelmed by the sheer magnificence of it. For it was nothing more nor less than the finishing of the painting of the professor's house. He would do it this very evening, alone and unaided, so that when Oswald arrived there with the dawn tomorrow morning he would find it done, and Robert, as his brother, would share the professor's gratitude. It would be one in the eye for old Oswald. It would be several in the eye for old Bertie.

But, though his spirits soared exultantly at the prospect, he did not overlook the practical difficulties. His mind went back to a recent occasion when, finding a tin of red paint in the garage, he had conceived the idea of painting the garden seat red during his family's absence in order to provide them with a pleasant surprise on their return. While the seat was only faintly coloured by the time they returned, William himself presented the appearance of a solid block of red paint, and gratitude played no part in the emotions with which they received their 'surprise' . . . He would be more careful this time. He opened the door of the tool shed and looked inside. Stacked in a corner was a heap of sacks that had once contained the various artificial manures and fertilisers with which Mr Brown was wont to dress his garden soil. He held them up one by one. Yes, they would afford a good protection. The largest one, tied round his waist, would cover him down to the feet, while one of the smaller ones would protect his shirt and jacket. A certain amount might fall on his face and hair, but that could easily be removed. He burrowed about a little longer and found a length of rope that could be used to tie round his waist and secure the armour to his person.

He laid them in a neat pile just inside the door then turned his mind to the consideration of his plan of action. He decided to wait till the guests had set off for the party, then make his way quietly and unobtrusively to the scene of his labours.

Still lurking in the shadow of the tool shed, he waited till Robert, wearing a new tie and new socks, his trouser creases pressed to a knife-blade sharpness, his shoes polished to a glass-like brilliance, the muscles of his face set and tense, emerged from the front door and made his way down the road towards the Bartons' house. Then, collecting his two sacks and his rope and bundling them under his arm, he set off across the fields to Ilfracombe Terrace. Keeping his eye on the road, he saw the figure of Oswald, spruced and shining to rival Robert, his face wearing the same set tense expression, treading briskly and purposefully towards the Bartons'.

Rowena was emerging from the gate of the professor's house as William reached it. It was clear that she, too, had taken considerable pains with her appearance, but she carried the effect with a less self-conscious air than Robert and Oswald.

'Hello, William,' she said.

'Hello,' said William.

'Where are you off to?'

'Oh, just – off,' said William vaguely.

'Well, enjoy yourself,' said Rowena and floated on down the road.

William watched her out of sight, then stood at the gate surveying the house. A long ladder stretched from the ground to the top storey. All the windows were painted except the one near which the ladder rested. Of that one corner only showed bright green. At that point the professor had evidently surrendered to his sciatica.

Withdrawing cautiously behind a bush, William unrolled and donned his sacks. He secured the longer one round his waist by the piece of rope. The other was conveniently rotten, so that he could push holes in it for his head and arms. Encased in sacking, he emerged warily from his hiding place. The garage door stood open and, just inside, he could see a can of green paint and a brush. Screwing up his courage, he crossed to the garage, took paint can and brush and began to mount the ladder.

All went well. The rooms he passed on his upward flight were empty. Evidently the professor's bedroom and the kitchen were on the other side of the house. Reaching the top window, he plunged the brush into the can of paint and sloshed it generously over the woodwork – so generously that glass, window-sill and the surrounding brick work as well as his own face, hair and armour of sacking all received lavish portions. He worked till he had covered the area within his reach, then, remembering the skylight, climbed cautiously from his ladder to the roof. Scrambling over a tile-covered peak, he found the skylight on a sloping part of the roof between the peak he had climbed and a further peak. Exhilarated by the adventure, upheld by the sheer joy of craftsmanship, he started sloshing paint over the skylight and the surrounding surfaces. The skylight was open a few inches and his efforts sent a stream of paint down on to the floor below.

'Oh well,' he consoled himself, 'I 'spect it needed a bit of dec'ratin' inside as well.'

Then, having finished the skylight to his own satisfaction, he turned his attention to the ridges of the roof on either side. He didn't see why they shouldn't be green, too, to match the woodwork. He set to work on them, at first merely covering the surface with paint, then, yielding to a sudden artistic impulse, describing squiggles, circles and little faces. Time slipped by. Dusk began to fall . . . He was interrupted by the sound of a loud tattoo on the front door below. He stopped to listen.

'I've come for the ladder from Clements',' he heard a man's voice say. 'They only lent it for a week an' it's up.'

'Oh, well, I suppose you can take it,' a woman's voice

WILLIAM WATCHED A MAN CARRY
THE LADDER TO A LORRY.

replied. ''E's in bed, anyway, so 'e wouldn't be able to use it
even if you left it.'

William heard the sound of the ladder being drawn down.
Peering over the ridge of the roof, he watched a man carry it
to a lorry at the gate and drive off with it.

Then he turned to consider his position.

He was marooned on the roof of a tall house with no means, as far as he could see, of escape.

He climbed down to the low parapet that surrounded the roof and looked over it. There was no convenient tree, no convenient drain pipe. Again he considered his position. Perhaps the roof of the next house would give him a better chance. It was a perilous journey, over sloping roofs and ridges, but he achieved it at last. Then, just as he was craning his neck over the parapet, reconnoitring the ground, he saw Miss Burnham and her friend enter the gate and make their way up the short drive.

They, too, had evidently been to the party.

'Such a pleasant evening, wasn't it?' said Miss Burnham.

'Yes. Charming people, the Bartons,' agreed her friend.

They entered the house. William continued to gaze over the parapet through the gathering dusk. There was no convenient tree or drain pipe here, either.

The front door was open and he heard the clear resonant voice of Miss Burnham.

'I'll be getting on with the supper, dear. I prepared it beforehand, all but the soup.'

'And I'll pop out to the post with some letters,' said the friend.

The friend emerged from the front door, then casually and by chance glanced up at the roof. Her mouth dropped open in surprise and she returned to the house.

'I've never noticed before, dear,' she said, 'that you had a gargoyle on the roof.'

'A what?' said Miss Burnham.

'A gargoyle . . . That carved head painted green.'

'That – *what*?' said Miss Burnham.

'Carved head painted green . . . Well, I saw it quite plainly. I know the light isn't very good, but you can't imagine a carved head painted green.'

'There's no such thing,' said Miss Burnham. 'I'll go and look. Stir the soup for me while I'm out, will you? I can't leave it. The directions say that it must be stirred continuously till it boils.'

William had hastily withdrawn his head by the time Miss Burnham looked up at the roof.

'There's nothing there at all,' she said when she returned.

'I tell you there *is*,' protested the friend. 'I saw it with my own eyes. You can go on with the soup now. I'm going to look again.'

It happened that Miss Burnham's friend had slipped off the high-heeled shoes that she had worn at the party and that were a little too small for her, and slipped on a pair of comfortable crêpe-soled shoes. Her footsteps made no sound and, looking up, she saw again the face of William, peering over the parapet, desperately seeking some way of escape.

'It *is* there,' she said triumphantly as she re-entered the house. 'As plain as plain can be. A carved head painted green. I tell you, one couldn't mistake it.'

'Go on stirring the soup. I'll look again,' said Miss Burnham.

The sharp click-click of her high-heeled shoes warned William of her approach and again she looked up at the plain unadorned line of the parapet.

There followed a short scene in which Miss Burnham and her friend came out one after the other, turn and turn about, to look up at the roof. The click-click of Miss Burnham's high-heeled shoes always warned William of her approach, while the soundless movement of the crêpe soles caught him unaware. An acrimonious note crept into the friends' conversation.

'Honestly, darling, you must be going blind.'

'I'm afraid you must have had too much to drink at the party, dear.'

'Well, *really*, if you imagine I've got Delirium Tremens on two glasses of sherry . . .'

Suddenly they saw Mr Lupton returning to his house. Mr Lupton, too, had been to the party.

'I don't care what happens to the soup,' said Miss Burnham. 'I'm going to get to the bottom of this . . . Mr Lupton!' she called.

Mr Lupton came in at their gate.

'Good party, wasn't it?' he said.

'A little too good in my friend's case, I'm afraid,' said Miss Burnham. 'Now, Mr Lupton, will you stand here and look up at my roof. Do you see a carved head painted green?'

'No,' said Mr Lupton.

'I don't now,' said the friend, 'but I certainly did before.'

The three stood looking up at the roof. William despairing of making a descent by way of Miss Burnham's house, was making his way, past chimney-pots, up and down tiled slopes, to Mr Lupton's roof, hoping for better luck there.

'None of us can see it, so it can't be there,' said Miss Burnham triumphantly.

'It was a trick of the fading light probably,' said Mr Lupton. 'Well, I'll be getting on.'

He walked out of the gate and in at his own gate. Absently he looked up at the roof. And there indisputably was what seemed to be a green painted head. He gave a shout of surprise and consternation. Miss Burnham and her friend came scuttling out of Miss Burnham's house.

'What is it, Mr Lupton?'

'I can see it, too,' he said. 'I can see it quite plainly.'

They joined him and stood gazing up at William. Paralysed by horror, William remained motionless, gazing down at them.

'Good Lord! It's incredible,' gasped Mr Lupton. 'I wonder – I wonder if it could be something in the drinks. I've half a mind to ring Mrs Barton up . . .'

'It might be a good idea,' said Miss Burnham adding bitterly, 'The soup, of course, will be completely ruined by now.'

Mr Lupton entered his house and the other two followed. Mr Lupton took up the telephone.

'Mrs Barton? ... Thank you for a wonderful party, Mrs Barton. I'm going to ask you a rather strange question, but – have you had any – er – complaints from your other guests?'

'Complaints?' said Mrs Barton.

'Yes, of – seeing things?'

'What things?'

'Well – er – green heads. Green heads on roofs. I know it sounds odd.'

'It sounds *most* odd,' said Mrs Barton.

'Miss Burnham and her friend and I have all seen them. I just wondered ... Oh, well, I'm sorry to have troubled you ... Yes, perhaps you're right. Strong black coffee and get to bed ... Thank you so much ... Good-bye.'

They emerged from Mr Lupton's house.

'It's gone,' said Miss Burnham, looking up again at the roof.

William had been taking stock of the situation. It was evidently no use going on from house-top to house-top. The journey was a dangerous one and it was unlikely that any of the others would afford a better means of descent. Crouching at the foot of a chimney-pot, he abandoned himself for a moment to despair. Must he spend the rest of his life crawling about among roofs and chimneys? Then his fighting spirit returned. The skylight of the professor's house! It was only a few inches open, but he could open it further. He would enter the house by the skylight, wait till the coast was clear, then creep down the stairs, out of the front door, and make his way home. His ever-ready optimism returned in full flood. There was nothing to worry about. He'd be safely back home in a few minutes now.

The return journey was slow and difficult – the slopes and

ridges seemed to have increased in size since he first tra-
versed them – but at last he reached the open skylight.

And then, just as he was putting out his hand to find the
inside catch that secured it, there came the sounds of revelry
from below.

Robert, Oswald and Rowena as well as a crowd of other
young people had still been at the party when Mrs Barton
received Mr Lupton's telephone call. But they couldn't stay at
the party after that. The party broke up in sudden disorder,
and the crowd of young people, headed by Robert, Oswald,
Rowena and Peggy Barton, came rollicking down the road to
visit the scene of the mystery.

'Either all three are completely sozzled or it's a poltergeist,'
said Peggy Barton.

They stood at the gate of the professor's house and gazed
up at the parapet of the roof.

'Well, there's nothing to be seen,' said Oswald.

Then Peggy Barton gave a scream.

'Look! The poltergeist!'

William, standing by the now open skylight, turned at the
scream. The moon was rising and its beams caught his
startled green-bedecked face. Without a moment's hesitation,
he plunged through the skylight.

'Good Lord!' said Oswald. 'Good *Lord*! I–I'd bet my bottom dollar it was William.' There was malicious glee and
unholy triumph in his voice. 'Your name's going to be mud in
this house, Robert, old chap, if it was.'

Robert had turned pale. He, too, had caught a fleeting
glimpse of the green-bedecked face and he, too, would have
bet his bottom dollar it was William.

'Come on!' shouted Oswald exultantly. 'Let's go in at the
front door and nab him.'

William, after letting himself down through the skylight,
found himself in a large attic with a sloping roof. There were

hiding places in plenty – boxes, trunks, packing cases – but William had had enough of hiding places. He wanted to get home. He opened the door and looked out cautiously. A short flight of steps led down to a half-landing. No one was about. The coast was clear. He descended noiselessly to the half-landing and looked down the main part of the staircase to the hall and front door. The coast was clear there, too. He was just beginning his cautious descent when suddenly the front door burst open and the revellers, headed by Oswald, appeared in the doorway.

Panic-stricken, William threw open the nearest door, flung himself into the room and closed the door behind him.

He found himself in a large bedroom. On the bed lay Professor Mayfield, propped up by pillows and wrapped in a tartan shawl. By the bed sat a harassed-looking young man, holding a sheaf of papers in his hand. The bed and the floor near the bed were strewn with papers. William noted that the papers were covered by sketches of large fantastic creatures, rather like prehistoric animals.

'I'm awfully sorry,' he panted.

But the professor had shot an arm out of the tartan shawl and was pointing at him.

'*There* he is!' he said, turning to the young man. '*That's* what I want.' His eyes, beneath thick bushy eyebrows, darted back to William. 'Don't move. Stay just where you are ... Now sketch him and make notes of the colour. The green streaked face. The green spiked hair. The green armour covering him from neck to toes. The green hands. The green tail (for the piece of rope, now sodden with green paint, with which William had secured his sacks, had somehow managed to curl itself round his feet). The things you've been doing are too large, too horrific. Nothing large can be really sinister. To be really sinister the creature must be small. Smallness is the essence of the sinister, and green is the essential colour of the sinister. Get him now just as he is, with that villainous scowl on his face.' William, stung by this description, altered his expression to what he imagined to be a polite smile. The professor gave a shout of delight. 'Better still! That fiendish grin! Get that fiendish grin quickly before it goes . . . Got it?'

'Yes,' said the young man.

He proceeded to sketch on a piece of paper, moving his eyes from William to his work.

The professor relaxed against his pillows.

'I owe you an explanation,' he said to William. 'I'd better make a full confession, I suppose. You see – this is not generally known but the secret is bound to come out sooner or later – under the name of Martin Morrow I write space fiction for the younger reader.'

'Gosh!' gasped William. 'Martin *Morrow*! They're smashing! They're super! I've read them all . . . Gosh, do you axshully *write* them?'

'I actually write them,' said the professor. There was a

WILLIAM GAVE WHAT HE IMAGINED WAS A POLITE SMILE.

touch of complacency in his smile. His work as an economist won him the praise of the greatest intellects of the day, but William's appreciation of his space fiction gave him more pleasure than their most enthusiastic plaudits. He enjoyed writing his space fiction and he was tired of economics. 'In my next book, I propose to introduce a creature of supreme and evil intelligence called Tonando. He has landed in Mars from some other planet and is laying it waste, exterminating the inhabitants or reducing them to a state of mechanical slavery. Those who land on Mars from our own planet escape only with their spirits broken and their bodies maimed. The book will be called "The Scourge of Mars". This' – he pointed to the young man – 'is my illustrator and the sketch he is making will form the frontispiece of the book.'

'Gosh!' said William. 'Is my picture goin' to be Tonando?'

'Your picture is going to be Tonando.'

'Gosh!' repeated William, a smile of ineffable bliss on his lips. '*Gosh!*'

'Now stand still for a few more minutes, please,' said the professor.

Suddenly there came a knock at the door and Rowena entered. Behind Rowena could be seen Robert and Oswald, behind Robert and Oswald could be seen the odds and ends of the party, behind the odds and ends of the party could be seen the anxious peering faces of Miss Burnham, her friend, and Mr Lupton.

'We're so sorry to interrupt you, Daddy,' said Rowena, 'but we saw someone – or something – coming in by the skylight window, and we've searched the whole house and—' Her eye fell on William. '*There* he is!'

'It *is* William,' said Oswald. There was quiet triumph in his voice.

The professor turned on the intruders with such a roar of fury that they melted swiftly and silently away.

Only Oswald stood his ground, while Robert hovered unhappily in the background.

'And what do *you* want, may I ask?' said the professor to Oswald.

'I think I ought to tell you,' said Oswald, who had made a pretty thorough examination of the premises in the limited time at his disposal, 'that this boy, William Brown, has splashed green paint all over the glass of the top window and over the surrounding brick work, that he has practically covered the skylight with green paint, disfigured the roof in its vicinity, and, not content with that, has left a train of green paint along the top landing in the house and green finger-marks all over the balusters . . .'

He stopped, quelled by the ferocious expression that had come over the professor's face.

'And what business is that of yours?' said the professor. His voice rose to a bellow. 'Take yourself off, sir.'

Oswald took himself off. The professor turned to Robert.

'And who is this young man?' he said in a tone of ominous politeness.

'This is Robert, Daddy, William's brother,' said Rowena. 'I–I was going to ask you if I could ask him to come to tea.'

The professor made an expansive gesture that swept the tartan shawl clean off the bed.

'Come to tea?' he said. 'By all means. Come to tea, come to lunch, come to dinner, young man. Any relation of Tonando, the Scourge of Mars, is welcome in this house.'

'Oh, Daddy, thank you,' said Rowena, retrieving the shawl.

Robert could only stammer incoherently. His feelings were too deep for words.

'And now leave us,' said the professor. 'Our sketch is not quite finished. We have serious work to do.'

'I'm sorry about the paint,' said William when the door had closed on them.

'Don't mention it. Don't mention it,' said the professor. 'What's a spot or two of green paint to dwellers in the stratosphere? . . . Yes, smile again. I particularly want the fiendish grin.'

The next morning William strolled down the village street. At the expense of much time and labour, with the assistance of Robert and to the accompaniment of impassioned maternal reproaches, he had been drenched in turpentine, soaped, scraped, scrubbed, scoured and released from his coating of green paint. Even after a night's rest his face still felt a little sore, and he was pleased to find that portions of green paint still adhered to his hands. It showed that the whole thing had not been a dream.

He had spent part of the tip that Robert had given him on a packet of monster humbugs. His cheeks bulged and his jaw moved rhythmically as, with a skill born of long practice, he manipulated one of the unwieldy morsels.

Turning a bend in the road, he met Bertie Franks. Bertie grinned at him maliciously.

'I bet you got in a row after last night,' he said.

'No, I didn't,' said William indistinctly through his monster humbug. 'Not much of one, anyway. Robert got me off.'

The malice of Bertie's grin intensified. He gave a mocking laugh.

'I bet Robert's not got much chance left, anyway, after that mess-up of yours.'

'That's what *you* think,' said William. 'Well, let me tell you that Robert's goin' there to tea.'

Bertie's mouth dropped open.

'Gosh, he isn't.'

'*An*' to lunch.'

'Gosh, he *isn't*.'

'*An*' to dinner.'

'*Gosh!*'

He knew when William was bluffing and he knew that he wasn't bluffing now.

'Oh, yeah?' he sneered. 'And who d'you think *you* are, anyway?'

William removed his monster humbug in order to give point and audibility to his reply. His features contracted into a startling grimace as he tried to assume the ferocious scowl and fiendish grin simultaneously.

'I'm Tonando, the Scourge of Mars,' he said.

Then his features returned to their normal positions and, replacing his monster humbug, he strolled on nonchalantly down the road.

# Chapter 4

# William's Thoughtful Act

'It's my mother's birthday on Monday,' said William, drawing his tongue with lingering relish over the bright red surface of a lollypop.

'What are you goin' to give her?' said Ginger.

'I'm goin' to give her a thoughtful act,' said William.

'A what?' said Henry.

Douglas, who had just put his lollypop into his mouth, made a sound suggestive of interest, query and surprise.

The four were sitting astride the roof of Ginger's tool-shed, enjoying a little relaxation after a game of Palefaces and Redskins in Coombe Wood.

'A thoughtful act,' repeated William. 'Well, I got her a jolly fine present las' year. I got her some sort of imitation mats with holes in for lace that looked jus' like real ones an' they must have been jolly good ones 'cause they cost a shilling an' then in the afternoon she sent me shoppin' an' I stopped at Jenks' farm 'cause they were havin' a rat hunt an' Jumble wanted to join in an' then I sort of forgot the shoppin' an' went home without it an' she said a thoughtful act was better than a present so I thought I'd give her a thoughtful act this year an' not bother with a present.'

'A jolly good idea,' said Ginger.

'It's cheaper, too,' said William simply, 'an' I haven't any money.'

'What are you goin' to give her for a thoughtful act?' said

Henry, licking the last remnant of lollypop from his stick and putting it behind his ear.

'I haven't quite thought it out yet,' said William. 'It's not as easy as it looks, thinkin' out a thoughtful act.'

'You could do some weedin' in the garden,' suggested Ginger.

'Or carry in a few coals,' said Douglas.

'Or do a bit of washin' up,' said Henry, removing the lollypop stick from his ear and taking an imaginary puff at it.

'If I'm goin' to do a thoughtful act,' said William emphatically, 'I'm goin' to do somethin' a bit more excitin' than *those*.'

'You could ask her what she'd like for a thoughtful act,' said Ginger.

'No, what's the use of that?' said William. 'A birthday present's got to be a s'prise. I thought once of fixin' up a shower over the bath. I could do it easy with a pipe from the tap an' a tin with holes in, but I knew they'd stop me the minute I started on it. Pity' – regretfully – 'that all the really excitin' thoughtful acts are things they won't let me do.'

'You could clean your shoes,' said Douglas, looking down at those battered mud-encrusted articles.

'Oh, shut up!' said William and, stung to resentment by the futility of the suggestion, gave the offender a push that sent all four of them slithering down from the roof on to the ground.

The resultant scrimmage brought them to the notice of Ginger's mother, who called Ginger in to lunch and unceremoniously dismissed the other three.

When William reached home he found his family already assembled for lunch. Mrs Brown's usually placid face wore an expression of gloom.

'Cheer up, darling,' Robert was saying.

'Nothing's as bad as it seems,' said Ethel.

'It is. It's worse,' said Mrs Brown. 'It's all very well for you to laugh. You persuaded me to take on this wretched job of secretary to the Village Hall Committee because you said it would give me outside interests and take my mind off household worries, and all it's done is to give me a whole crop of outside worries that make the inside ones seem like child's play.'

'What's the trouble, my dear?' said her husband.

Mrs Brown looked at him with an air of patience strained beyond endurance.

'I've told you,' she said. 'I've told you over and over again. You never listen to a word I say. It all goes in at one ear and out at the other . . . Well, I'll tell you again. Are you listening?'

'Yes,' said Mr Brown.

'With the ear it goes in at,' said Ethel.

'Well, there's dry rot in the Village Hall platform and Heaven only knows how much it's going to cost to get it out, and if we don't get it out Mrs Bott or Mrs Monks will just disappear through it one of these days while they're opening something.'

'Don't get it out, then,' said Mr Brown.

'And we'd arranged to have the whole place done up, starting next week,' said Mrs Brown, ignoring his interruption, 'and the Fortescues had promised to store all the stuff in their old stables at Brent House—'

'What stuff?'

'*Masses* of stuff. Crockery and theatrical properties and trestle tables and tea urns and *cupboards* full of stuff, because the cupboards have to be painted, too. And then when the Fortescues managed to sell their house at last I took for granted that the new man who bought it—'

'Mr Tertullian Selwyn,' said Robert.

'Yes . . . Anyway, when I wrote to him to ask him if he

would he just wrote back to say that he wouldn't. And when I sent him a copy of the dry rot appeal he just ignored it.'

'Oh, yes,' said Robert. 'I met the Vicar in the Post Office and he was talking about him. He told the Vicar that he didn't want to have anything to do with local people or local affairs.'

'Who does he think he is, anyway?' said Ethel disdainfully.

'I've never heard of him before,' admitted Robert, 'but evidently he's a big noise in artistic circles. He began life by qualifying as an architect but he's never practised. He's designed ballet settings and ballet costumes and theatrical settings and theatrical costumes and won prizes for embroidery.'

'How sickening!' said Ethel.

'Why did he come here if he feels like that?' said Mrs Brown.

'He wants the artistic inspiration of rural surroundings,' said Robert, 'but he doesn't want contact with rustics. We're all rustics in his eyes. He says that contact with rustics would blur his artistic integrity . . . And, anyway, he's in a state of nervous jitters at present.'

'Why?' said Ethel.

'He deserves them,' said Mrs Brown.

'Oh, he poured it all out to the Vicar. He wants his name to be handed down to posterity and he's afraid that nothing he's done so far will hand it down, so he's entered for a competition for the design of a new theatre somewhere or other to house the new experimental drama and till the results come out he – well, he's in a state of nervous jitters.'

'Fellow ought to be in a madhouse,' said Mr Brown.

William had been applying himself busily to a large plateful of stew. Having taken the edge off his appetite, he turned his attention to the conversation that was going on around him.

'An escaped lunatic's got the strength of ten men,' he

announced. 'Ginger said so. His mother's char-woman's brother knew someone that once met an escaped lunatic – well, he turned out not to be one in the end, but—'

'William!' said Mrs Brown, noticing her younger son's appearance for the first time. 'Did you wash your face before you came to the table?'

'I wiped it over,' said William on a casual note and with a hint of dignity in his voice.

'I said, did you *wash* it?'

'D'you mean, did I put it right into water?' temporised William.

'Yes, of course I do.'

'Well, listen,' said William earnestly. 'Cats are s'posed to be clean animals an' *they* don't put their faces right into water when they wash 'em.' He gave his short sarcastic laugh. 'Well, it's news to *me* if cats put their faces right into water when they wash 'em. I mus' say *I've* never seen a cat puttin' its face right into water when—'

'*William*!' said Mr Brown. 'Stop arguing and go and wash your face.'

William stopped arguing and went and washed his face. Returning, he was sent back to improve the process. Returning again, he was sent back to improve the process still further. In an attempt to cover the whole business with ridicule, he plunged his head into water and arranged his wet hair in a series of spikes. He was disappointed that none of his family commented on it when he re-entered the dining-room. Mrs Brown was still holding forth on her grievances.

'So I suppose we shall just have to go on and on with Bring and Buy Sales and Whist Drives and White Elephant Sales and never getting anywhere . . . Oh, well, it's Mrs Barlow's little effort this afternoon and she's thought of something quite new. She's got a make-up expert coming to speak on make-up. Everyone pays two and six entry and the expert comes for nothing so there isn't any trouble about getting White Elephants and things together.'

'You certainly seem to spend the greater part of your life rounding up the creatures,' said Mr Brown sympathetically.

William finished his second helping of apple pudding and rejoined his friends in Coombe Wood.

'Your hair looks jolly funny,' said Ginger.

'Yes, it's nearly all washed away same as my face,' said William bitterly as he smoothed back his spikes. 'Gosh! Jus' think of it! Me takin' all this trouble givin' her a thoughtful act an' all she does back to me is carry on about my face!'

'You've not given her one yet,' Henry pointed out.

'No, 'cause I've not got one thought out yet. It's jolly hard work thinkin' out a thoughtful act. My brain's jus' about worn out with it. An' I bet' – darkly – 'all that washin' didn't do it any good, either. Well, your brain's somewhere *inside* your face, isn't it, an' washin' on an' on an' on at it, same as they made me do, mus' wear it away. Stands to reason. There's a *disease* called water on the brain an' I bet I've got it an' it's all their fault an' they'll be jolly sorry when it's too late.' He paused to contemplate a pleasant mental picture of his family weeping round his sick bed. 'Yes, they'll be *jolly* sorry . . . You never hear of a *cat* with water on the brain. They've got more sense. They've got this *instink* I kept tryin' to tell 'em about.'

'You don't look ill,' said Douglas.

'That's nothin' to go by,' said William. 'Anyway, you can't *see* my brain, can you, you chump! I bet it's wringin' wet.'

'Are you goin' to go on thinkin' about this thoughtful act this afternoon?' said Ginger.

'No,' said William. 'I'm goin' to give my brain a bit of time to dry out before I start usin' it again.'

'What'll we do this afternoon, then?' said Henry.

'Let's play Palefaces an' Redskins,' said William, abruptly

abandoning his grievances. 'Come on. You be the Paleface ridin' round your ranch an' Ginger an' Douglas be the Redskins ambushin' you an' I'll be the Sheriff that comes in the nick of time to snatch you from the jaws of death. Come on. Let's start.'

The game was fast-moving and eventful. The Paleface was scalped, boiled and eaten several times. The Sheriff was kidnapped and tied to a tree with a trail of dynamite attached to his pullover, but in the end Sheriff and Paleface routed the Redskins and a formal trial was held at which William was judge, jury and prosecuting counsel and which suddenly and unaccountably turned into a circus with Douglas and Henry as lions and William and Ginger as lion tamers.

When William reached home Robert and Ethel were there, but Mrs Brown had not yet returned.

'Good Lord!' said Robert, eyeing his young brother with an expression of distaste. 'Must you go about looking like something that's been dug up out of the mud?'

'Me?' said William indignantly. 'Gosh! I washed myself enough at lunch to last for *months*, didn't I? An' I've got a jolly funny feeling comin' on an' I shouldn't be s'prised if it's not water on the brain. I shouldn't be s'prised I'm not injured for life. I—'

Then Mrs Brown entered.

She looked coy and bashful and radiantly pretty. Her cheeks were delicately tinted, her eyelashes darkened, 'eyeshadow' enhanced the blue of her eyes and lipstick gave to her lips an allure with which nature had never endowed them.

'I've been made-up,' she said simply. 'The woman used me as a model.'

'Heavens above!' said Robert helplessly.

'You're a menace,' said Ethel. 'I shall never dare invite a boy friend to the house again.'

'Oh, I'll wash it off,' Mrs Brown reassured her, 'but' – she glanced at the mirror over the fireplace – 'it does look rather nice, doesn't it? What do you think of it, William?'

'I like you better old,' said William politely.

Then Mr Brown came in and stood in the doorway, open-mouthed with amazement.

'I've been made-up,' said Mrs Brown again. 'She used me as a model.'

'It's positively staggering, my dear,' said Mr Brown, partly gratified, partly outraged by the sight of his glamorised wife. 'I've never seen you look like this in all my life before.'

'And you never will again,' said Mrs Brown, 'so make the most of it.'

'What do you feel like?' said Robert.

Mrs Brown glanced again at her reflection in the mirror.

'It makes me think I've wasted my life,' she said. 'It makes me think of all the things I haven't done or been to. I've never been to the South of France or Ascot or a Buckingham Palace Garden Party or – I can't think of anything else.'

'We'll think of them for you,' said Robert. 'You've never been on a Polar expedition.'

'Or to the Olympic Games,' said Ethel.

'As a matter of fact I've always wanted to go to the Olympic Games,' said Mrs Brown. 'I took a passionate interest in them in my younger days . . . Well, I'll go and unmake my face now.' She turned at the door with a sigh. 'We only made three pounds. What's that to a platformful of dry rot? I'm sorry to keep harping on it but I can't get it off my mind.'

William slipped over to Ginger's house. Ginger was in the garden.

'I say, Ginger, I've got an idea for that thoughtful act.'

'What is it?'

'Well, she said she wanted to go to the South of France and a Buckingham Palace Garden Party—'

'Well, you can't take her there. Gosh! You'll get in an awful row if you do.'

'I know, but she said she wanted to see the Olympic Games, too.'

'Well, you can't take her there, either. 'Least, you'd have to wait for *years* an' it'd be a bit late for a birthday present for Monday.'

'Oh, do shut up makin' objections an' *listen* to me,' said William testily. 'You start makin' objections before I've had time to open my mouth. I've got to have quiet to talk in, haven't I, same as other people.'

Ginger was startled into silence by this novel view of William's eloquence, which had been known to hold its own against the most nerve-shattering uproar.

'All right,' he muttered. 'All right. Go on.'

'Well, listen,' said William. 'We've got to do somethin' to cheer her up 'cause of this dry rot she's got on her mind. We can't axshully take her to the Olympic Games, but we can *do* the things they do at Olympic Games. We can practise them till we've got them all right an' then bring her along to watch them. We'll find out jus' what they do an' do the same things an' I bet it'll be as good as the real ones.'

'Well, nearly,' agreed Ginger and added, 'P'haps.'

'We shan't be able to get it fixed up tomorrow 'cause of it bein' Sunday, but we'll meet after school on Monday an' practise the games an' then fetch her along to see 'em. It won't matter it bein' in the evenin'. It'll still be her birthday. Gosh! It's goin' to be jolly excitin', isn't it?'

'Yes, I 'spect it'll be that,' said Ginger.

The four met after school on Monday. Henry, informed of the plan, had come armed with exhaustive information. There were few subjects on which Henry could not arm himself with exhaustive information.

'They have running, jumping, boxing, fencing, wrestling, shooting, cycling, rowing, tennis, football, polo, gymnastics an' throwing the hammer. I looked it up in my father's encyclopaedia.'

'We can't do quite all those,' said William, a little taken aback. 'Not *quite* all . . . We can do some of 'em, of course. We'll pick out the best.'

'We could run an' jump an' box an' wrestle,' said Ginger.

'An' cycle an' fence,' said Henry. 'We could use walking-sticks for fencing.'

'We could play polo if we had a horse,' said Douglas. 'I've always wanted to play polo.'

'Throwing the hammer's all right,' said William. 'We've got a new hammer at home. I bet I could borrow it for a bit without anyone knowin'.'

'Where'll we have the practice?' said Ginger. 'In the field by the old barn?'

'No,' said William. 'Everyone can see that from the road. Someone might see an' tell her about it an' it's got to be a s'prise.'

'There's that bit of land behind Brent House,' suggested Henry. 'No one'll see us there.'

'But it b'longs to Brent House,' said Ginger doubtfully. 'That new man that's come to live there might make a fuss.'

'No, he won't,' said William. 'My fam'ly was talkin' about him. He's called Mr Selwyn an' he isn't int'rested in rustics an' we're rustics so he won't be int'rested in us. Come on. Let's c'lect the things an' start the practice.'

'I'll bring my cycle,' said Henry.

'I'll bring walkin'-sticks for fencin',' said Ginger.

'If I can find a horse I'll bring it for polo,' said Douglas.

'I'll bring our new hammer,' said William.

They returned a little later with the various implements.

Douglas arrived first. They found him gazing through the hedge at the smooth back lawn of Brent House.

'That man doesn't seem to be anywhere about,' he said, 'so we needn't worry.'

'Haven't you brought anythin' for the games?' said William sternly.

Douglas stooped down and picked up a croquet mallet and ball.

'Yes, I thought these'd do for polo if we could find a horse, but I couldn't find one. I looked everywhere.'

'Oh, you're bats!' said William. 'Now come on. Let's start. We'll start with throwin' the hammer.'

'No, with fencin',' said Ginger.

'Cycling,' said Henry.

'Polo,' said Douglas. 'I don't see that a horse is all that necess'ry.'

They leapt into their parts with enthusiasm and for a few minutes the scene was one of wild confusion – Henry wobbling about on his bicycle, holding the handle-bar with one hand and flourishing a walking-stick with the other as he carried on a fencing match with Ginger on foot, William throwing his hammer, Douglas playing a complicated game with croquet mallet, ball and imaginary horse. Then William called the team to order.

'We can't do it this way,' he said. 'It'll never get to be a thoughtful act, the way you're goin' on.'

They gathered round him breathlessly, Henry and Ginger still carrying on a spirited if erratic fencing match.

'Now listen,' said William, assuming his generalissimo air. 'We'll do 'em all in turn an' we'll do 'em *prop'ly*. We'll *practise* 'em. We'll start with throwin' the hammer an' I'll do it first an' then the rest of you do it. Now watch.'

They watched.

He swung the hammer round his head then sent it

THE HAMMER FLEW THROUGH THE AIR, OVER THE HEDGE
INTO THE GARDEN OF BRENT HOUSE.

flying . . . It flew through the air, over the hedge of the garden of Brent House, and vanished from sight.

Immediately there came the sound of a yell of anguish, followed by a groan.

'Gosh!' gasped William.

They crept to the hedge and stood, a small apprehensive group, peering through it.

A man lay prone in the middle of the lawn. About a yard from his head lay the hammer that was obviously the cause of his downfall.

'We've killed him,' said Ginger solemnly. 'We've killed Mr Selwyn.'

'We'll get in an awful row if we have,' said Douglas. 'There's lors against it.'

'Murder,' said Henry with a certain morbid relish.

'Let's go an' have a look at him an' see,' said William.

They made their way to the lawn through a small green gate in the hedge and stood looking down at the man who lay there unconscious. He had sparse red hair, bushy red eyebrows and he wore a raincoat buttoned up to his neck.

'He's dead all right,' said Ginger.

Henry knelt down by the form and inspected its face with a professional air.

'I think he's still breathin',' he said. 'Jus' a little, anyway.'

'P'r'aps they go on breathin' for a bit,' said Douglas. 'Same as hens. Hens go on runnin' round in circles after they're dead.'

'Well, he's not runnin' round in circles,' Henry pointed out.

'No, but that doesn't prove he isn't dead,' said Douglas.

'We'd better fetch a p'liceman,' said William. He had gone rather pale. 'I'll take the hammer with me an' show him.'

'No, leave it alone,' said Henry. 'You mustn't touch anythin' on the scene of the crime.'

'It's *my* hammer,' said William, a touch of resentment showing through his dejection.

'It's the blunt instrument,' said Henry.

'Come on, then,' said William, adding gloomily, 'Gosh! Who'd have s'posed a thoughtful act could have turned into this!'


Police-constable Higgs, strolling down the village street, paused for a moment or two to gaze at the Post Office window. There was seldom any alteration in the arrangement of the Post Office window, but it varied the monotony of Police-constable Higgs's 'beat' to note what alteration there was . . . Yes, they must have sold the pink and white apron because a tea-cosy, highly frilled and of a particularly lurid shade of purple, stood in its place. And the toy crane had gone. A pair of white sandshoes stood there instead. A nice little crane, it had been, with a neat little pulley and chain.

Police-constable Higgs had studied it daily during the last few weeks. He felt a certain regret at its disappearance. And that tray with a picture of the Tower of London on it was in a different place. Police-constable Higgs wished they'd sold it instead of the crane. It had been there since Christmas and it was getting on his nerves. He turned from the window to find a row of four small boys confronting him. He knew them, of course. Knew them only too well, the young monkeys!

'Now then!' he said briskly. 'What are you up to, you young rascals?'

'We've come to report a crime,' said Henry.

'We've killed Mr Selwyn,' said Ginger.

'I hit him on the head with a hammer,' said William.

'Doin' a thoughtful act,' explained Douglas.

'Now look here!' said Police-constable Higgs. 'I've had enough cheek from you kids an' I'm not takin' any more. Off with you!'

'He's lyin' in the garden,' said Henry. 'We've not moved anythin' on the scene of the crime.'

'He was still breathin' jus' a bit when we left him,' said Ginger.

'When you *what*?' said Police-constable Higgs.

'When we left him,' said Ginger.

'After we'd killed him,' said Douglas.

'Left *who*?' said Police-constable Higgs.

'Mr Selwyn,' said Henry. 'He lives at Brent House, you know.'

'Lived,' said Douglas.

'I didn't *mean* to hit him on the head with a hammer,' said William.

Something pale and stricken in William's face impressed Police-constable Higgs. He hesitated for a moment, then,

'Well, come on,' he said at last, 'and if you're up to any of your monkey tricks—'

'It's not a case of monkey tricks,' said Henry impressively. 'It's a case of trag'dy stalkin' abroad an' claimin' its victim.'

'Now then!' said Police-constable Higgs faintly.

They walked in silence down the road. A feeling of nervousness was creeping over Police-constable Higgs. He could cope with the usual routine of his police duties, but anything beyond them unnerved him. He was relieved to see the stalwart form of his cousin Bill advancing down the road towards them.

'Come along and give me a hand, will you, Bill?' he said.

Bill looked at him suspiciously.

'If you're going to change your hens back to that other shed you can do it yourself,' he said. 'I can still feel the place where that Buff Orpington bit me on the ear.'

'No, this may be a spot of real trouble,' said Police-constable Higgs.

Bill brightened.

'Suits me,' he said shortly as he joined the company.

They crossed the piece of waste land, where bicycle, fencing sticks and croquet mallet lay hastily abandoned, and went through the small green gate to the back lawn of Brent House. The recumbent form of the man in the raincoat still lay on the grass. They gathered round, looking down at it.

'There he is,' pointed out William unnecessarily.

'Mr Selwyn,' said Ginger.

'The corpse,' said Henry.

Police-constable Higgs scratched his head.

'That isn't Mr Selwyn,' he said.

'Who is it, then?' said Ginger.

'Search me!' said Police-constable Higgs.

'The tangled web of mystery,' said Henry.

Suddenly the recumbent form sat up, blinking distractedly.

'Crikey!' it said. 'Where am I?'

'In the garden of Mr Selwyn's house,' Police-constable Higgs reassured him.

'I hit you on the head with a hammer,' said William as if in further reassurance.

The man scrambled to his feet, looking round in a panic-stricken fashion.

'I'll be off,' he said. 'I ain't done nuffin. I tell you I ain't done nuffin. I'll be off.'

'Hold him Bill,' said Police-constable Higgs sharply.

Through the french windows that opened on to the lawn he had suddenly caught sight of a startling object. A couple of wildly waving arms. A writhing form tied to a chair by a piece of rope. A face consisting of two glaring eyes and a large enveloping gag. Bill's iron grasp held the man in the raincoat while Police-constable Higgs strode across the lawn to the french windows. He entered the room, approached the struggling form, severed the rope with his penknife, and then cut through the gag, releasing a scream that made him blench and step hastily backward.

Mr Selwyn rose to his feet and shook himself. He was a small man. He wore a fawn suit, a heavily embroidered yellow satin waistcoat, hair longer than convention demanded, a low collar and flowing Byronic tie. His face – not unnaturally – wore an expression of extreme agitation.

'Where is he?' he said on a high-pitched hysterical note. 'Where is the blackguard?' then, seeing the group on the lawn, ran out of the french windows to join them. He plunged his hand into the pocket of the man's raincoat and brought out a gold cup, beautifully decorated with figures of sea-horses in bas-relief. He clasped it to his breast ecstatically. 'My Luck! The Luck of the Selwyns!' He turned to Police-constable Higgs, who stood watching, stupefied by amazement. 'This was brought from Italy by an ancestor of mine in the sixteenth century. It's supposed to be the work of Cellini himself. And ever since then it's been the Luck of the family. Nothing has gone wrong with us while we've had it

in our possession, and, during the time it was out of our possession, nothing went right. It's of inestimable value. I keep
it generally in the bank. I took it out the day I posted my
plans for the experimental theatre and I took it out again this
morning because I expect to hear the results of the competition this evening. I knew that, unless I had my Luck with me,
the result would be failure. I could only hope for success if I
had my Luck with me. The brute must have known of this.
He surprised me, gagged me, bound me, took my precious
Luck and then – What happened? What happened? Tell me
what happened.'

'WHERE IS THE BLACKGUARD?' CRIED MR. SELWYN
RUSHING OUT ON TO THE LAWN.

'I hit him on the head with a hammer,' said William.

'Oh, you brave boy! You heroic boy!' said Mr Selwyn with tears of gratitude in his voice. 'How can I thank you? How can I ever thank you?'

'Now then! Come on! Come on!' said Police-constable Higgs, rallying his scattered forces. 'Come on to the Police Station, all of you.'

Mr Selwyn addressed him with an air of hauteur.

'I'm expecting an important telephone call in a few minutes' time. Also I wish to have a word with this heroic boy. We will join you at the Police Station shortly.'

'I ain't done nuffin,' wailed the man in the raincoat. 'Someone must have planted it on me. 'It me on the 'ead with an 'ammer an' planted it on me. I've got a crule 'eadache an' I feel tired.'

'Don't worry,' said Bill. 'You'll get a nice long rest.'

Mr Selwyn ushered his guests into a room that made them open their eyes wide in amazement. The walls were hung with brightly coloured masks, antique weapons, examples of 'modern' art, signed photographs or caricatures of theatrical celebrities, and designs of stage settings. The floor was covered with a white carpet woven into intricate coloured patterns of squares, circles and triangles. A shelf that ran along one wall was filled with models of theatrical décors, and a glass case contained 'souvenirs' of famous actresses and ballerinas in the form of gloves, caps, belts, fans, shoes. An enormous gilt couch of obviously theatrical origin stood cheek by jowl with a small Georgian writing-desk and a Victorian what-not, while a table of aggressively contemporary design supported a sheaf of faded wax flowers under glass. A bird cage containing a canary hung from the centre of the ceiling and an old ship's figurehead was fixed on the wall between the windows. Mr Selwyn's embroidery frame stood in front of a baronial fireplace and samples of his work lay about the room in the shape of screens and cushions.

'And now, my brave, brave boy,' he said, turning to William. 'Tell me how you discovered the plot and how you foiled it. You heroic child! You must have risked your life to save my Luck.'

The telephone on the desk rang and he flung himself upon it, still clutching his 'Luck' to his breast.

' . . . Oh, thank you, thank you, *thank* you . . . ' they heard him say.

He put back the receiver and turned to them, his thin face quivering with joy.

'I've won the competition,' he said. 'It could only have

happened if I'd had my Luck with me. If that villain had taken it I should not have had the slightest chance of success . . . They liked my drawing. It had, they said, a touch of the bizarre that the others lacked. I have, as you may have noticed' – his hand swept round the room – 'a strong sense of the bizarre, but without my Luck it would have been of no help to me . . . And now tell me, tell me, tell me. Tell me everything, my gallant boy.'

Deeply embarrassed, his gallant boy told him everything. It was an incoherent story – made still more incoherent by the additions and corrections of the other three – but, miraculously, as it seemed, Mr Selwyn understood it. And Mr Selwyn liked it. It appealed to his sense of the bizarre. His cackling laughter rang out as he listened.

'You see,' said William, 'you wouldn't let her keep that Village Hall stuff in your stables—'

'But I will, I will, I will,' broke in Mr Selwyn. 'Of course I will.'

'An' she was worried about this dry rot in the platform an'—'

'I'll be responsible for that,' said Mr Selwyn, brandishing his Luck in an expansive gesture. 'Let her not concern herself with that for another minute. That shall be my responsibility . . . And now let us proceed to the Police Station and then to your home.'

Mrs Brown, on going to the front door in answer to a prolonged and thunderous knock, was surprised to find William standing on the doorstep and behind him a small thin man in a rather startling waistcoat, holding a gold cup to his bosom.

'Many happy returns of the day, Mother,' said William ceremoniously.

'Yes, dear,' said Mrs Brown, her voice faint with astonishment. 'You wished me that this morning.'

'An' I said I'd give you your present this evenin'.'

'Yes, dear.'

'Well, here it is,' said William waving a hand at his companion and moving to one side.

'I'm the thoughtful act,' said Mr Selwyn as he stepped over the threshold.

# Chapter 5

# William's Television Show

William lay outstretched on the hearthrug in his bedroom, surrounded by a sea of nondescript pieces of paper, his hair ruffled, his brow furrowed, his face streaked with lead pencil.

Henry, Ginger and Douglas sat on the floor near him, each holding a piece of paper and studying it with a puzzled expression.

They had arranged to call for William and go into the woods for a game of Cowboys and Indians, but had found him engaged in literary composition.

'I'm writin' a play,' he said, 'an' I can't come out till I've finished it. I've nearly finished it.' He gazed at the sea of papers and added complacently. 'I write 'em jolly quick. You can read what I've done if you like. It's a jolly excitin' one.'

They took up the papers and read them with growing bewilderment. William's writing was illegible at the best of times, and the idea of numbering the pages had never occurred to him.

'Doesn't make *sense* to me,' muttered Ginger.

'Oh, shut up,' said William. 'It's you that don't make sense.'

'I can't read a single word on this page,' said Douglas.

'Well, that's the bit of paper the marge was wrapped in. It's jolly diff'cult, writin' on marge.'

'An' I bet the meat was wrapped in this one,' said Ginger.

'Well, what's a bit of blood?' said William. 'It makes it more excitin'. It shows there's a murder in it.'

'What's a g-n-a-v-e?' said Henry.

'Gosh!' said William. 'Have you never heard of a knave? You don't know English, that's what's wrong with you. Gosh, you might be foreigners, the way you talk.'

'What's this oculist doin' in it?' said Ginger.

'What oculist?' snapped William.

'The one that lives in a cave by the sea an' bites people's legs off.'

William threw a glance at the page.

'It's an *octopus*,' he said testily. 'Can't you *read*? Gosh! I don't s'pose anyone's ever wrote plays for people as ign'rant as what you are. Now stop talking an' let me finish it.' His face resumed the ferocious scowl that denoted concentration and his tongue protruded as his stubby pencil scored its way heavily across the paper. 'Allas my dume is ceiled I am knored by the pangs of hunger and serve me rite for being a villun of the deepest die steaped in krime I've a jolly good mind to reppent and see if the grashius king will spair my life.'

'There!' he ended. 'That's as far as I'm goin' to write it.'

'Tell us about it,' said Henry, adding tactfully. 'The papers have got in a bit of a muddle.'

'All right,' said William, sitting back and drawing his fingers through his hair, leaving it standing up in a jagged formation of spikes. 'It's a jolly excitin' play. It starts with a man out of hist'ry that's an outlaw an' he kidnaps this other man—'

'What other man?' said Ginger.

'This old man with a beard,' said William impatiently. 'Anyway he kidnaps this man an' takes him to the wood an' chains him to a tree an' leaves him to starve to death an' he'd got nothin' to eat but the bark of the tree an' he ate it till it nearly drove him mad an' then he escaped—'

'How?' said Douglas.

'He unscrewed the screw that the chain was fastened to the tree with. He hadn't thought of doin' that before. It came to him quite sudden. Then he met this outlaw an' this outlaw was goin' for him, but he remembered that he'd got a wooden leg where this oculist – I mean octopus – had bit it off, so he unstrapped it an' gave the outlaw a bash on the head with it an' left him for dead but he wasn't dead – he was only pretendin' to be – an' he got up an' c'lected the other outlaws an' they took a dreadful oath of vengeance—'

'It's not goin' to be easy to act,' said Henry doubtfully.

'I've got in a muddle already,' said Douglas.

'I wish you'd shut up an' let me get on with it,' said William. They subsided again into silence. 'Well, this old man with a beard went home an' c'lected all his friends an' one of them was a chimney sweep, but he wasn't a chimney sweep really, he was the king in disguise, an' they had a jolly good fight with the outlaws an' they were jus' gettin' conquered when this king threw off his disguise—'

'How could he?' said Henry. 'You can't throw off soot.'

'Well, he did, an' shut up,' said William. 'An' then this man that'd got the secret plans—'

'What man?' said Ginger.

'The one that's a spy from a foreign country that'd come over disguised as a bus conductor—'

'You never said anythin' about him.'

'Well, you've *read* it, haven't you?' said William testily. 'Gosh! You've *read* it. Can't you read or what's the matter with you? I gave it you to read an' now you say you don't know anythin' about it. You've not got any sense, that's what's wrong with you . . . Well, this man disguised as a bus conductor—'

'Couldn't you have him disguised as a Dutch boy?' said Douglas. 'I've got a Dutch Boy's costume. I had it for Victor Jameson's fancy dress party.'

'No,' said William firmly. 'I've got a bus conductor's set an' a bus conductor's more nat'ral than a Dutch boy an' if you're goin' to keep on int'ruptin''—

'Well, never mind,' said Henry soothingly. 'Go on telling us about it.'

'Well, axshully there's two spies,' said William, 'an' the one disguised as a bus conductor murdered the other an' hid him in a cellar but the p'lice found the blood on the cellar steps an' caught him, but he escaped an' hid up with this out-law in the octopus's cave an' then the king came along and they had a fight an' captured the outlaw an' put him in a dun-geon to starve to death till he repented so he starts repentin'.' He consulted the sheet of paper. 'He says, "it serves me right for bein' a villain of the deepest dye, steeped in crime." He means he's been a bad man.'

'Why can't he say so, then?' said Ginger.

''Cause he's out of hist'ry,' said William with the air of one whose patience is almost exhausted. 'I told you he was out of hist'ry, didn't I? So he's got to talk hist'ry language, hasn't he? Stands to reason.'

'Is that the end?' said Henry.

'It's as far as I've got,' said William. 'I'm not goin' to write any more. I'm sick of writin'. We can make up the words of the rest as we go along. Anyway, there's not much more. He turns good an' the king lets him out of the dungeon an' he stays good an' ends up as a Member of Parliament. An' this foreign spy that was disguised as a bus conductor met his fate all right. He kept teasin' the octopus an' in the end it got mad an' ate him.' He was silent for a few moments then heaved a deep sigh and ended, 'It's a jolly good play. We'll act it.'

'When?' said Henry.

'Where?' said Ginger.

'Why?' said Douglas.

'Tomorrow in the old barn,' said William, ignoring Douglas's question.

'Who'll come to watch it?' said Ginger.

'Everyone,' said William. 'Everyone'll come to watch it.'

'I bet they won't,' said Douglas gloomily. 'Not with television. They all watch television plays now. They don't want real ones.'

A light broke out over William's countenance.

'*Tell* you what!' he said. 'I've got an idea. We'll make it a television play. Gosh! It'll be better than any ordin'ry television play.'

'How?'

'Well, in television plays you only see the pictures of the people an' in this one you'll see the real people. Gosh! It'll beat an ordin'ry television play hollow. We'll call it a live television play an' I bet they'll all come to it.'

The others were silent, surrendering to the feeling of helplessness and bewilderment that was apt to possess them as they were swept along on the current of William's enthusiasm.

'It's one of the best ideas I've ever had,' said William.

'How'll we start it?' said Henry.

'We'll put up a notice,' said William.

He took a crumpled piece of paper from the floor, wrinkled his brows again ferociously for a few moments, then sent his stubby pencil scoring across it in a sudden access of inspiration.

There will be a reel live tellyvishun sho not just pitchers here tomorro afternune at three oklock diffrent from ordinry tellyvishun a knew invention of William Browns the first time evver seen by ennybody in the hole world fre to all.

cined William Brown.

'There!' said William triumphantly. 'I bet everyone'll want to come to it. Come on. Let's fix it on the door of the old barn.'

Still gripped by the feeling of helpless bewilderment, they followed his plunging figure down the stairs.

At the foot of the staircase the open door of the sitting-room revealed the figures of Ethel, Archie Mannister and Oswald Franks.

'Can't you come downstairs without shaking the whole house?' said Ethel as the whirlwind procession passed the door. 'Shattering our nerves like that!'

'I've got more important things to think of than your nerves,' said William, knocking over the umbrella stand in his haste, then flinging open the front door and leading his band at breakneck speed down the path to the gate.

'No wonder she's got nerves,' he said scornfully as he swung the gate open, 'sitting round all afternoon showing off to that old Oswald an' Archie!'

'What have they come for?' said Ginger.

'They keep comin,' said William scornfully. 'They can't stay away. They like the look of her face. They don't know how awful she is really.'

Oswald and Archie had each called at the Browns' house to ask Ethel to accompany him to the Young Conservatives' dance as his partner. They had not planned a joint expedition. It was an unkind stroke of fate that had delivered both of them on the Brown front door step at the identical moment. They had stood there, glaring at each other in silence, till Ethel herself opened the door and ushered them into the sitting-room with the expression of demure sweetness and wondering innocence that she reserved for such occasions.

They had tendered their request almost in the same breath, and Ethel, who had learned by experience how to extract the last ounce of savour from these situations, was keeping them on a maddening see-saw of alternate hope and despair. She really hadn't decided whether to go to the dance or not. She thought she had another engagement for that evening but couldn't quite remember what it was. Actually she was afraid that she was booked for the dance. Several people had asked her to go with them, but really, till her plans were clearer and till she knew definitely whether she would be able to go to the dance or not, it was not worth making final arrangements.

She gave more encouragement to Oswald than to Archie. Archie cherished his hopeless passion for her day in day out, year after year after year, with wearisome monotony; Oswald had spurts of rebellion that made him more interesting. Goaded beyond endurance, he would suddenly transfer his attentions to Dolly Clavis or Peggy Barton or Marion Dexter or Rowena Mayfield, which lent the situation a certain piquancy. Lately he had been escorting Dorita Merton to and from the tennis club and taking her out in his car at the week-end, but Ethel had known it wouldn't last, because Dorita was going through a highbrow phase and wanted to talk about William Empson and T. S. Eliot and the symbolic and neo-romantic when Oswald wanted to talk about himself. So she hadn't been altogether surprised to see him pace into the sitting-room side by side with Archie.

'Well, shall we leave it open for the present?' said Oswald. 'Perhaps you'll let me know when you see your way more clearly . . .'

'Yes, just give me a ring,' said Archie.

'I'll bring my car for you, of course,' said Oswald.

'I'll fetch you in a taxi,' said Archie after a brief mental survey of his car's latest exploits.

'How good of you!' said Ethel, fluttering her lashes demurely.

She was tired of talking about the dance but she wanted to tease them just a little longer. She had several well tried recipes for teasing her boy friends. One of the most successful was to praise an absent boy friend, extolling virtues in him that those present did not possess.

'George brought us some eggs this morning,' she said, turning her innocent dreamy gaze from Oswald to Archie, from Archie to Oswald.

'Eggs?' said Archie.

'George?' said Oswald.

'George Bell,' said Ethel. 'Yes, eggs. The Bells keep hens, you know, and it's such a treat to get eggs fresh from the hen. I thought it was so kind of him. He's just made a new hen-house.'

'Hen-house!' said Oswald, enduing the words with a mixture of detachment, amusement and contempt.

'Hen-house!' said Archie with a startled expression.

'Yes. It's beautifully made. I do so admire a man who can make things. I don't suppose either of you have ever made a hen-house in your lives, have you?'

'The occasion,' said Oswald with dignity, 'has never arisen.'

'Well, not a hen-house,' admitted Archie, looking round in a hunted fashion. 'Not *exactly* a hen-house.'

'Daddy was talking about it the other evening,' said Ethel. 'He was saying that in these days people have lost the art of making things. Craftsmanship is practically dead. Most men are so helpless nowadays. The type of man I admire is the type who can *create*, who can make things with his hands. Practical things, I mean,' she added hastily, remembering Archie's studio full of unsold paintings. 'Things like – well, things like hen-houses. I told George how much I admired him for it. And the eggs, of course, are delicious.'

She stifled a yawn and looked at the clock. The guests rose reluctantly to their feet.

'Well, I mustn't take up any more of your time,' said

Oswald. 'I'll hope for the best in the matter of the dance.'

'I'll – I'll get the tickets in any case,' said Archie.

'Oh, I've got tickets,' said Oswald with a hollow laugh.

Archie hung back as they passed through the hall.

'You're coming to tea with me tomorrow, aren't you, Ethel?' he pleaded.

Ethel hesitated.

Every week Archie asked her to tea with him in the cottage where he carried on his chequered career as an artist. Every week Ethel refused the invitation. But last Tuesday had been her birthday, and he had given her a box of chocolates of such dimensions that, before she quite realised what she was doing, she had accepted the invitation.

'I suppose so,' she said in a tone that markedly lacked enthusiasm.

She accompanied her guests to the hall, picked up the scattered umbrellas and set the umbrella stand to rights.

'That *boy*!' she said. 'One never knows what he'll be up to next.'

There was a gratifyingly large attendance at the old barn for the television show. Some of the viewers had come in a spirit of criticism, some in a spirit of curiosity, some in simple quest of entertainment. All had come with a touching confidence in William's ability to break the monotony of life.

The first arrivals were the Thompson twins – recent additions to the neighbourhood. They were solid compact children, with upturned noses, curly hair and long mischievous mouths, called Launcelot and Geraint. Arabella Simpkin came next – thin and spindly and determined-looking – dragging by the hand her two-year-old brother, Fred. Frankie Parsons came next, wearing his usual air of self-sufficiency. Maisie Fellowes followed, looking more like Queen Victoria than ever. Victor Jameson, Jimmy Barlow, Ralph Montague,

'I'M GOING TO MAKE A SPEECH,' SAID WILLIAM. 'SO SHUT
UP AND LISTEN.'

Ella Poppleham, Caroline Jones and the rest jostled and
pushed each other through the doorway and all raised a cheer
as William mounted the precarious packing-case that served as
his platform.

'Now listen, everyone,' he said. 'Shut up an' listen. I'm
goin' to make a speech, so shut up.' The tumult partially subsided. 'We're goin' to give you a new sort of television show
an' you've not got to pay anythin'. It's goin' to be *free*.'

'And dear at that, I shouldn't wonder,' put in a shrill voice.

'Shut up, Arabella Simpkin,' said William. The tumult
began again and he raised his voice to quell it. 'Shut *up*, I tell

you . . . Now listen. You're goin' to see a new television show diff'rent from any other television show you've ever seen in your lives before.'

'I can't see any set,' said Frankie Parsons. 'Where's the set?'

'There isn't any set,' said William. 'That's what makes it diff'rent from any you've ever seen. It's diff'rent from any other television show in the whole world.'

'Yes, I bet it'll be that all right,' said Arabella Simpkin with a short harsh laugh.

'I'm not talkin' to you, Arabella Simpkin, so you can jus' shut up. Now listen, everyone. *Listen . . . !* In ordin'ry television shows you only see pictures of people, but in this television show you're goin' to see the real live people same as you don't in ordin'ry television shows. Gosh! It's a jolly sight more excitin' than jus' seein' *pictures* of 'em, isn't it? It's the mos' wonderful invention that's ever been invented an' it's been invented by me. A television show with real live people in it, 'stead of jus' pictures of 'em, 'an you're jolly lucky to be the first people to see it.'

The audience was silent for a moment or two. Dimly they felt that there was a weak spot in the argument but so infectious was William's enthusiasm, so persuasive his eloquence, so wholehearted his own belief in the unique properties of his invention, that they were carried away despite themselves. Even Arabella Simpkin joined in the cheer that followed and the twins turned head over heels and began to butt each other in the stomach, which was their usual way of giving vent to their feelings.

'We're goin' to start with a play,' announced William, 'an' don't forget that you're seein' real live people in it that you'd only see pictures of in an ordin'ry television show an' that it's the greatest invention that's ever been invented . . . It's a jolly excitin' play, too. It's made up by me an' written down by me an' acted by me. Well, Henry an' Ginger an' Douglas are doin' a bit of it but it's mos'ly acted by me. It's called "The Kidnapper's Downfall" or "The Bloody Steps" or "The Octopus's Revenge" by William Brown. It's got a lot of names 'cause a lot of things happen in it. Now are you ready?'

The audience gave an answering cheer and the play began.

Judged solely as a play, it was not an unqualified success. The cast had held one rehearsal only but, with the optimism of the creative artist, who sees his work as he had intended it to be rather than as it actually is, William had been satisfied.

'You needn't bother to remember the axshul words,' he had said carelessly. 'Jus' go on actin'. It's such an excitin' play that you've only got to go on actin' it an' rememberin' what happens next.'

'Well, *that's* not goin' to be easy,' Douglas had said.

'Oh, shut up makin' objections,' replied William. 'I'll tell you what to say if you can't remember it. I could act it all by myself, come to that, without makin' all this fuss.'

And William did, in effect, act it all by himself. He had piled up such properties as he could collect in a corner of the old barn and the viewers watched enthralled as he plunged into the corner, donned his false beard, returned to black his face with soot, plunged back to put on his kingly crown, struggled manfully if unavailingly with the eight sticks that were intended to transform Ginger into an octopus and finally, flinging aside his bus conductor's uniform, joined combat with Henry, Ginger and Douglas, as the king's forces.

It was at this point that the viewers could restrain themselves no longer. The twins started the rush towards the part of the floor that had been set aside for the stage.

'Go it, William!' they shouted. 'Go it, ole William!' and proceeded to butt Henry, Ginger and Douglas in the stomach with well-aimed blows of their bullet heads.

The rest of the viewers joined in, shouting lustily, supporting William's side or Ginger's as the fancy took them. It was a glorious mêlée and it lasted till both sides were too much exhausted to continue it any longer. Then William, an impressive figure, his face streaked with soot, his bus conductor's 'set' hanging disjointedly about him, his false beard still adhering to one ear, rose breathlessly to address his audience.

'Well, it was a smashin' play,' he said. 'There's more of it really but I forget how it goes on, so we'll stop now an' go on to the next thing. The next thing's "Animal, Vegetable or Mineral" but with real live people in it like me an' Henry an' Ginger an' Douglas, 'stead of jus' pictures of people same as you get in ordin'ry television . . . I'll show Henry an' Ginger an' Douglas somethin' an' they've got to guess what it is . . . Now we'll start, shall we?'

The viewers, exhilarated by the recent performance, yelled agreement and William, diving once more into his heap of properties, brought out a small fluffy object – most of it concealed by his hand – and held it up.

'What's that?' he said.

'A pineapple,' said Douglas.

'It isn't,' said Henry.

'It is.'

'It isn't.'

'It is.'

'It isn't.'

'It's a feather duster,' said Henry.

'It isn't,' said Ginger.

'It is.'

'It isn't.'

'It is.'

'You're doin' it jolly well,' said William, looking proudly at his team.

'What is it, then?' they said to him.

William wished to prolong the excitement. There was to be no tame ending to his 'Animal, Vegetable or Mineral' programme. He stuffed the object back into his pocket.

'Take it off me an' I'll tell you,' he shouted.

They set on him and, nimbly dodging them, he began to run round the barn, pursued by his team. And again, with shouts of glee, the viewers joined in. Again the barn was full of scuffling, wrestling, shouting, leaping, running children.

'All right,' said William at last in a muffled voice from beneath the seven or eight viewers who were sitting on him. 'I'll tell you now.'

He crawled from under them and drew a handful of hay, straw and feathers from his pocket.

'It's a bird's nest,' he said. 'It wasn't a good shape to start with – I bet the bird that made it didn't know much about makin' nests – and it got all bashed up in my pocket.'

They seized and scattered it, ramming it down each other's necks, fighting for fragments of it, throwing it into the air, laughing hilariously.

William scrambled to his feet. The entertainment had been so successful that he was reluctant to bring it to an end.

'What else do they do in ordin'ry television?' he said.

The twins stopped butting each other in the stomach and turned to him.

'They knock down houses,' said Launcelot.

William stared at him.

'They – what?' he said.

'Knock down houses,' said Geraint.

'I *bet* they don't,' said William.

'Well, they did it once. Someone was telling us about it the other day. They knocked people's houses down when they were out an' waited to see what they said when they came home an' found them knocked down.'

'*Gosh!*' said William.

'Then they gave 'em money an' they didn't mind,' said Launcelot.

'I bet my fam'ly would,' said William.

'Well, your fam'ly doesn't know how to act then,' said Launcelot. 'Television people don't mind. They don't mind anythin' as long as they get money given 'em, don't television people.'

'Where does the money come from?' said William with a puzzled frown.

'The people that get up the television show pay it,' said Geraint.

'Oh,' said William blankly.

'Come on,' shouted Launcelot excitedly. 'Let's go an' knock a house down.'

'Yes, let's go an' knock a house down,' cried the viewers, stampeding towards the door.

'Hi! Wait a minute,' said William. He felt that the situation was getting a little out of hand. 'We haven't got anythin' to knock it down with, anyway.'

'We'll get things,' yelled Launcelot and Geraint.

'Yes, we'll get things,' echoed the viewers joyfully.

They poured out of the door of the old barn and scattered over the countryside.

'They'll be comin' back with shovels an' saws an' hammers an' things,' said Douglas morosely. 'I bet they won't leave one house standin' in the village by the time they've finished an' we'll have to pay for the whole lot.'

'No, they're only goin' to do one,' said Ginger. 'I bet television people only did one at a time.'

'Yes, but what about this money?' said William anxiously. 'I dunno that we've got enough money to pay for a house.'

'How much have we got?'

'I've got sixpence,' said Henry.

'I've got sevenpence halfpenny,' said Douglas.

'I've got threepence,' said Ginger.

'I've got fourpence and a farthing,' said William.

Henry wrestled with the sum in silent concentration for a few moments.

'It's one and eightpence three farthings,' he said at last.

'It's a lot of money,' said Ginger.

'Yes, but I don't know that it's enough to pay for a house,' said William. 'I dunno how much they cost.'

'We'll try'n' fix on a little one,' said Ginger.

'I dunno that it wouldn't be better to stop this television show altogether,' said Douglas. 'Couldn't we say there's been a technical hitch?'

'It's too late,' said Henry.

It was too late. The viewers were swarming back across the field, waving saws and hammers and spades and garden forks. Launcelot carried a pair of pruning shears, Geraint an alpenstock. Frankie Parsons had a coal hammer, Caroline Jones a croquet mallet. Arabella Simpkin carried an ancient umbrella and Fred the small wooden spade that had accompanied him on his seaside holiday last month.

Halfway across the field they stopped.

'Come on!' they shouted. 'We're ready.'

William and the others ran down to join them and the whole body trooped back again towards the village. William's doubts had faded. The carefree exhilaration of the viewers had communicated itself to him, and he was beginning to think that the whole thing was his own idea. He seized a large fallen stick from the ditch that bordered the road and walked at the head of the ragged formation, brandishing it above his head.

They stopped outside the gate of the Hall and surveyed the stately edifice – wings, porticoes, pediments, turrets and gables.

'That's too big,' said William. 'We'd never get that down. It'd take us weeks, anyway.'

They moved on to the Vicarage. That, too, seemed to present an impregnable front to the world.

'That'd take too long, too,' said William.

'We could have a bash at it,' said Launcelot wistfully.

'Yes, let's have a bash at it,' said Geraint.

'No,' said William firmly. 'It's too big. Come on.'

The band rollicked down the road. At Archie's cottage they stopped and crowded round the gate, surveying the ramshackle structure with interest.

'I bet we could get that down,' said Launcelot.

'I bet we couldn't,' said Victor Jameson. 'It's got roses climbin' up it. Climbin' roses have got thorns stickin' out all over 'em. I once helped my father cut some pieces out of one an' it was like bein' shot at by bows an' arrows.'

'But *look*!' shouted Frankie Parsons. 'Look at that hen-house.' They looked at the hen-house. It stood on the lawn – a brand new shining hen-house.

'Gosh!' said William. 'It wasn't there the last time I came along the road.'

'Let's knock it down,' said Launcelot. 'It'll be easier than an ordin'ry house an' I bet it'll do jus' as well.'

'Yes, if we start on a hen-house it'll give us practice an' we can work up to ordin'ry houses gradually,' said Geraint. 'Come on. Let's knock the hen-house down.'

'He'll see us from the window,' objected Douglas.

'Well, we can't do it if he's in,' said Launcelot. 'That's the point of it. They've got to be out. Then you knock their houses down an' wait till they come back to see what they say an' give 'em money.'

'I bet it didn't cost more than one an' eight pence three farthings,' said William. 'Not much more, anyway . . . Come on. Let's see if he's out.'

They crept up to the cottage. Had Archie been in the cottage he would have witnessed the strange sight of a row of heads appearing suddenly at the bottom of each window in turn and rising simultaneously to inspect the interior of the room. But Archie apparently was not in the cottage. There were the usual signs of Archie's occupation – a kitchen sink piled high with used crockery and saucepans, a studio scattered with tubes of paint, paint brushes, palettes, half-covered canvasses and odds and ends of Archie's wearing apparel; but of Archie himself there was no sign.

'That's all right, then,' said William, throwing his doubts to the winds and assuming command of the situation. 'Douglas can stay by the gate an' let us know when he's comin' an' the rest of us can start on it.'

With hammers, spades, garden forks and shovels the viewers started on it. They hit and prodded and knocked and banged. Victor Jameson, throwing aside his poker, hurled his small but solid person upon it. Frankie Parsons wielded his coal hammer with such effect that he dealt himself several blows on the head for every one that reached the hen-house. Arabella Simpkin beat on the wooden side with her umbrella in an imperious manner as if demanding entrance, while Fred, dissociating himself from the whole proceedings, set to work making mud pies on a near-by flower bed with his wooden spade.

A tremor seemed to run through the shed at the first attack; then gradually it yielded to the assault. Gaping holes appeared as the thin frail wooden sides caved in before the attackers. The attackers redoubled their blows, hurling themselves and their weapons on it in a frenzy of excitement as the gimcrack structure collapsed into a heap of broken wood.

And then from the heap of broken wood there rose a pale and haggard face. Chips of wood adorned head and beard. Blood oozed from a jagged cut on the forehead. It opened its mouth and emitted a bleating sound.

'It's haunted!' screamed Arabella Simpkin.

'Archie!' gasped William.

\* \* \*

Archie had had a trying day. It happened that an enterprising itinerant salesman had bought up a bankrupt stock of sectional hen-houses of unusually inferior quality and had conceived the bright idea of disposing of them at enhanced prices by door to door canvassing. He had only found two purchasers in the village and one of them had been Archie. Archie had at first resisted the salesman's oily persuasiveness.

'It wouldn't be any use to me,' he had objected. 'I don't keep hens.'

The man waved the objection aside.

'You don't need to keep hens,' he said. 'Hens keep themselves. With a hen-house like this and a few scraps you'll have eggs enough to feed the whole village. And think of the interest of the thing.'

Archie thought of the interest of the thing, saw himself taking baskets of eggs to Ethel – bigger and better eggs than George Bell's hens could ever produce. He thought of Ethel's gratitude and the many opportunities for little chats with Ethel that the situation would provide.

'We deliver it free of charge,' said the man.

'But I don't know how you put it together,' protested Archie. 'That's going to be the difficulty.'

'Not at all,' said the man. 'It's simplicity itself. A child could do it. Full directions are given with it. An infant in arms could understand them. And you'll be surprised at the quality of the thing. All your friends will admire it. It's a piece of really fine craftsmanship.'

And that, of course, sent Archie's mind to what Ethel had said about craftsmanship the day before. He imagined Ethel admiring his hen-house, telling her friends about it, lauding his craftsmanship . . . It went to his head. He weakened, yielded, paid the money, and the next morning found the

'IT'S HAUNTED!' SCREAMED ARABELLA SIMPKIN.
'ARCHIE!' GASPED WILLIAM.

flimsy sheets of wood that formed the sections lying on his front lawn together with a badly-typed leaflet of instructions. The heading of the leaflet informed him yet again that the erection of the thing was simplicity itself and that a child could do it.

A child may or may not have been able to do it, but Archie couldn't. He wrestled with the instructions and sections alternately till he was in a state bordering on frenzy. Then he sent for old Amos, a local ancient who performed occasional odd jobs in the village at his own time and pleasure. Sometimes he came when you sent for him and sometimes he didn't. Sometimes he stayed to finish the job and sometimes he didn't. He liked to go to the Red Lion for his pint at twelve-thirty in the morning and, whatever stage the job had reached, twelve-thirty would see him ambling out of the gate and down the road towards the Red Lion. He was a small man with a bald head, a round wrinkled face, luxuriant grey whiskers and a squint. His sole contribution to any conversation was the word 'Ar'. He could put innumerable shades of meaning into it, but the word itself never varied.

Archie, strung about with nails and sections and the bits of string that had tied the sections together, almost wept with joy when he saw the small squat figure entering the gate. Amos carried his tools in a bag. Amos had two tools – a hammer and a pair of pincers. He knocked nails in with the hammer and pulled them out with the pincers.

'You see, Amos,' said Archie, unfolding the leaflet of directions. 'You fix it like this. I mean, it tells you here how to fix it . . . '

'Ar,' said Amos, scratching his bald head in a puzzled fashion.

'It must mean something,' said Archie desperately. 'I've read it and I can't make head or tail of it, but it must mean something. I mean, there must be *some* sort of meaning in it, don't you think?'

'Ar,' said Amos doubtfully.

'You see,' said Archie, 'there are letters pencilled on the wood and they're supposed to fit into each other. Look! There's an A on this piece and an A on that piece. Well, there *must* be a meaning of some sort if only one could find it.'

Amos examined the pieces and a light broke out over his round wrinkled face.

'Ar,' he said triumphantly.

And then they set to work. When they had got the floor in place, Archie, standing on the floor, held the sides in position while Amos hammered them together. They fixed the three sides and the roof. There only remained the fourth side.

'That's grand,' said Archie, his heart singing with happiness. 'Now there's only the last side. I'll hold it like this.'

He stood on the floor of the hen-house, holding the fourth side, while Amos hammered in the nails from the outside. As the last nail was driven home the church clock struck the half-hour. Half-past twelve . . .

'Ar,' said Amos, collecting his tools.

And then suddenly in a flash the full horror of the situation burst upon Archie.

'Hi! Amos!' he called.

'Ar,' said Amos from the gate.

'Amos!' called Archie with rising panic. 'I've got nailed up in it. Let me out.'

'Ar,' said Amos from the road.

'Amos!' shouted Archie. 'Come back. Let me out.'

Amos's 'Ar' was a distant breath upon the wind. He was half-way to the Red Lion.

'Amos!' called Archie wildly. '*Amos!*'

There was no answer.

Panic swept over him. The only door to the hen-house was a tiny opening by which the inmates were supposed to go in and out on their daily activities. He was imprisoned. He was imprisoned in a hen-house on his own front lawn. It had never occurred to him to move the thing to a less conspicuous position; he had erected it on the spot where the salesman had deposited the sections. The future loomed before him, black with menace. Sooner or later he would have to be released. The story would get round and the whole village would know about it. He seemed already to hear the bursts of mocking laughter that would pursue him for the rest of his life.

It would never be forgotten. He would never live it down. Wherever he went – through the length and breadth of England – the story would follow him. Titters, sniggers, bursts of mocking laughter. The man who had nailed himself up in a hen-house on his own front lawn. Ethel would go to the dance with Oswald Franks. They would talk of nothing else. They would rock and roar with laughter. The whole world would rock and roar with laughter.

Perspiration poured down his brow at the thought. All he wanted to do was to creep into a hole and stay there for the rest of his life, but, imprisoned as he was, he couldn't even do that. He would have welcomed the onset of any fatal disease, but even in his agitation he could detect no fatal symptoms.

He hurled himself against the sides of the shed but they resisted the assaults. He tried to crawl out of the tiny door but his head became jammed and it was only after many efforts that he managed to free it. He called 'Hi!' and 'Help!' but no one heard him. Then he succumbed to despair and sat crouched in a corner of his shed, facing the grim alternatives of death by slow starvation or a lifetime of public ignominy.

His despair was increased by the realisation that Ethel was coming to tea and that not only would he have no opportunity to go out and buy cakes for her, but that she would find him – if she found him at all – nailed up in a hen-house on his front lawn.

He didn't know how long he had crouched there before he heard the sound of approaching footsteps and, almost immediately, the impact of some weapon on the walls of his prison. He waited in a turmoil of apprehension, relief and perplexity. The frail match-board sections splintered into fragments, the roof fell on his head, a saw caught him on one cheek . . . and daylight came flooding through the chinks. He rose from the ruins, gasping and spluttering, and looked about him.

The viewers had fled in panic. Only William, Henry, Ginger and Douglas stood their ground.

'I say, Archie,' said William hoarsely, 'I'm terribly sorry.' He dug his hand into his pocket and brought out the one and eightpence-three-farthings. 'Will this be enough?'

But Archie wasn't listening. He was burrowing in his own pocket and bringing out a ten-shilling note.

'I can't tell you how grateful I am, William,' he said brokenly. 'You – you saw it happen, of course, and brought along these friends of yours to rescue me. I'm more grateful than I can say . . . and – and you won't tell Ethel, will you?'

'No,' said William, concealing his bewilderment as best he could and pocketing the ten-shilling note. 'No, we won't tell Ethel.'

'Not much good as a hen-house now,' said Henry, surveying the heap of splintered fragments.

'I don't want it as a hen-house,' said Archie fervently. 'I don't want the thing at all. I've had enough of it to last me the rest of my life.'

'What happened?' said William.

'I got caught up in it,' said Archie. 'It closed round me like a net. It was a ghastly experience.'

'It'd make jolly good firewood,' said Douglas.

'We could bash it up a bit more,' said Ginger.

'Yes, do,' said Archie, brightening as he suddenly saw the means of disposing of all traces of his ignoble plight.

They set to work with Archie's kitchen chopper till only a heap of small broken pieces lay on the lawn.

'That's all right now, isn't it, Archie?' said William. 'You can pile it up somewhere, can't you? D'you mind if we go now? We want to start on the ten shillings.'

'Not at all,' said Archie.

His face beamed with delight. He was a free man. The nightmare was over.

The four boys trooped down the road towards the sweet shop. Archie got busy with his wheelbarrow, carting load after load of 'firewood' round to the back premises of his cottage.

He was just carting the last load when Ethel arrived.

'What on earth's that?' she said.

'Oh, just firewood,' said Archie nonchalantly. 'I thought I'd get some in ready for the winter. It's as well to get firewood in during the summer, you know, when you can get it at summer prices.'

Ethel looked at him with a new respect. One would hardly have expected Archie to think of firewood at all, much less firewood at summer prices. He was perhaps less vague and impractical than she had imagined.

Then Archie remembered his tea-less cottage and followed up his advantage.

'I thought it might be a good idea to go out to tea,' he said airily. 'We could go to The Yellow Lizard if you like. It would make a nice change.'

The Yellow Lizard was a new up-to-date roadhouse that had recently been opened on the other side of Hadley.

Ethel's spirits rose. She thought of the teas that Archie was wont to serve to visitors in his cottage. Despite his frantic preparations, the tea was generally tepid, the milk sour, the cakes stale and the biscuits crumbled. Local tradesmen had formed the habit of unloading their more dubious wares on Archie.

'That would be lovely,' she said sweetly.

'I'll drive you there,' said Archie in a sudden burst of optimism.

'You've got a cut on your forehead,' said Ethel.

'Yes,' said Archie. 'I banged against a shed.'

'What shed?' said Ethel.

'Oh, just a shed,' said Archie.

He went to get out his car. Archie's car was the most

temperamental car within a radius of a hundred miles. There were days when, full of the joy of life and the lust for adventure, it charged head-on into everything it met. But today was not one of those days. Today it progressed demurely along the road in a dreamy contemplative fashion, only occasionally rearing up playfully as Archie applied the brakes or let in the clutch.

'You'd never guess what I saw in Oswald Frank's garden this morning,' said Ethel as they sped along the road.

'What?' said Archie.

'The most ghastly hen-house I've ever seen. Simply made of matchwood. Run up anyhow. Too clumsy and cheap-looking for words. It'll blow to pieces in the first gale. And the idiot had bought it from a man at the door. Can you imagine anyone being idiotic enough to buy a hen-house from a man at the door? After all I said yesterday about craftsmanship and workmanship . . . to go and buy a ready-made, ramshackle thing like that! And to buy it from a man at the door. Isn't it idiotic!'

'Idiotic!' agreed Archie happily.

Turning the bend in the road they met William, Henry, Ginger and Douglas. They were eating ice creams and lollypops. Their pockets bulged with giant humbugs, acid drops, pear drops, mint fancies, almond delight . . .

The eyes of William and Archie met for a fleeting second. They exchanged the ghost of a wink.

# Chapter 6

# William Does a Bob-a-Job

'We're gettin' on with it jolly well,' said William.

'Not too bad,' admitted Ginger, ''cept for the ones that shut the door in our faces soon as they saw us.'

William took his 'Bob-a-job' book from his pocket and studied it complacently.

'Well, we've done all the ones we did all right. They were jolly pleased with us. But' – his expression clouded over – 'I'm getting tired of weedin', aren't you?' He studied the card again. 'Gosh! They've *all* been weedin' so far.'

'Well, it's taught us which are weeds an' which aren't,' said Ginger.

'Yes, but it's goin' on an' on,' grumbled William. 'Anyone'd think there wasn't anythin' in the world but weeds. I'd like to do somethin' a bit more excitin'. There isn't any *adventure* in weeds.'

'Well, what sort of adventure d'you expect for a bob-a-job?' said Ginger.

'Someone might set us to find a missing will,' said William, 'or hunt for clues after a burglary or track down a spy – or help 'em with a space journey or somethin'.'

'Well, they won't,' said Ginger. 'Not for a bob-a-job.'

'Anyway, let's say we'll do anythin' but weedin' the next place we go to,' said William.

'All right,' agreed Ginger. 'I'm about sick of 'em, too.'

They had decided to confine their bob-a-job operations to

the rows of new houses that skirted the village, avoiding the older inhabitants, who, they considered, might be unduly prejudiced against them. And so far everything had gone well. Householders had thrown satisfied glances at flower-beds cleared of weeds, had signed the cards and handed over their shillings without demur. But William's enthusiasm for weeds, never very great, was flagging. 'They're all right for those that like them,' he said gloomily, 'but I'm beginnin' to feel I never want to see another weed as long as I live. I can't think why anyone ever started 'em.'

'Well, where shall we go next?' said Ginger.

They stood and looked about them. A neat little road, shady and inviting, led off the main road.

'Let's try that,' said William, adding dispiritedly, 'but I bet they all grow nothin' but weeds.'

They walked down the road, inspecting each garden as they passed it.

'Too many of them there,' said William, eyeing bitterly the groundsel and toadflex and mare's tails that flourished luxuriantly among the thin rows of antirrhinum and lobelia. 'Seems as if they trained 'em to shoot up as soon as they see us comin'.'

At last they reached a garden that showed only clear brown earth between its ordered rows of plants.

'Gosh!' said William. 'You can hardly b'lieve it, can you? Come on! I bet there'll be somethin' a bit more excitin' than weedin' to do here.'

A vague-looking old lady with white hair and a pleasant, rosy, wrinkled face opened the door to them.

'Bob-a-job!' announced William in a loud stern tone, fixing on her the fierce scowl with which he was wont to proffer his services.

'Oh, yes . . . How very kind of you! Do come in.'

She led them down the little hall to the kitchen. A cup of tea and a biscuit stood on the table.

'I was just going to have a cup of tea before I started out to do my shopping,' she said. 'I expect you'd like something before you set to work, wouldn't you?'

She opened a cupboard and brought out two bottles of orange squash and a tin containing biscuits and cakes. They were biscuits with sugar tops and cream insides and a large assortment of delicious-looking cakes.

'Now sit down and make yourselves at home,' she said, getting out two glasses and plates. 'My name's Miss Risborough, by the way. What are your names? . . . William and Ginger? . . . What nice names! Now help yourselves. The more you eat the better I shall be pleased. I had some people to tea yesterday and this was left over from tea and I'd like to get it finished.'

'Gosh!' said William faintly.

None of his other employers had provided refreshments, much less refreshments on this scale.

'I'm so glad you've come,' said the old lady in a friendly confidential tone. 'I was getting all worked up about things as one does when one has no one to tell one's worries to.'

William dived into the tin and emerged with an almond slice.

'Gosh, this looks good.'

'Bags me the jam tart!' said Ginger.

'All right! All right!' said William severely but indistinctly through his almond slice. 'Have a bit of *manners*, can't you?'

'It's silly of me to worry, of course,' said the old lady, sipping her tea thoughtfully. 'It's always silly to worry . . . but I've used that right of way for so long and it's such a handy short cut to the bus stop.'

'It's not jam,' said Ginger. 'It's lemon curd, but it's jolly good . . . What's a right of way?'

'It's weighin' things right,' said William. 'That new man at the sweet shop doesn't even *try* to. He stops puttin' them on

soon as the scales begin to wobble 'stead of goin' on till they
go down with a bang same as he's s'posed to by lor. I once
told a p'liceman about it but he didn't take any notice. He was
prob'ly in league with him.'

'No, no, dear,' said the old lady. 'A right of way gives you
the right to pass over somebody else's property. You see,
when first I came to the house there was a field at the bottom
of my garden and I had a right of way through the spinney of
trees at the end of the field that led out to the road just by the
bus stop. It saved me a long walk by the road. And when the
man who owned the field sold it for building he made it a condition that I should keep my right of way. He was a kind man,
you see, and he wanted to save me that long and tiring walk to
the bus stop . . . Have you tried the coco-nut buns? I made
them myself.'

'Yes,' said Ginger. 'They're smashing. I once hit a coco-nut
at a fair but it didn't come off. It jus' waggled.

'I've heard they glue them,' said the old lady. 'The thing I
used to like most when I went to fairs was knocking the pipe
out of the man's mouth. I did that three times on one afternoon.'

They gazed at her with deep respect.

'An' what happened to this right of way?' said William,
plunging his hand into the tin and bringing up a brandy snap.
'Did they dig it up or somethin'? I've never had one of these
before.' His voice sounded faint and muffled. 'They're super.'

'I'm so glad, dear. It's an old family recipe . . . No, they
couldn't take my right of way from me because it's legally
mine, but they're being most unpleasant. The people who
built the house, I mean. There's no reason why they should
object because it just goes through the little spinney of trees at
the bottom of their garden and my walking through it to the
bus stop doesn't hurt them at all, but there are two dreadful
boys who do all they can to stop me.'

'What do they do?' said William, discovering a cream bun at the bottom of the tin and setting to work on it.

'They lay booby traps and things. They dug a big hole yesterday and covered it over with brambles and undergrowth for me to fall into. And the day before that they put wet paint all along the top of the little gate I have to open. I'm going round by the road today, though it takes so much longer. I think I shall have to give up using the right of way altogether . . . And I've got another worry, too, but I won't waste your time with that. It's very good of you to have listened so patiently to my right of way worry . . . And now, if you've finished the cakes – yes, I'm so glad to see you have – perhaps you'll come into the garden and let me tell you what I want you to do.'

They followed her out of the kitchen door into the back garden. It was a pleasant shady garden with a herbaceous border, rose beds and a little lawn.

'Gosh!' said William, gazing around, his eyes widening in horror.

'Yes, dear,' said the old lady placidly. 'Weeds! Aren't they dreadful! They're simply everywhere. I've managed to clear the front garden, but I haven't had time to start on the back and, as you see, it's just choked with them . . . Now here are two trowels and a gardening basket so you can set to work at once and see how many you can get rid of before I return from my shopping.'

William gulped.

'You – you've not got a missin' will you'd like us to look for, have you?' he said.

'No, dear,' said the old lady, looking a little puzzled.

'Or – or clues or anythin'?' said William earnestly. 'If you've had a burglary lately we could hunt for clues.'

'No, dear,' said the old lady, looking still more puzzled. 'I haven't had a burglary.' She smiled. 'Just your little joke, isn't it, dear? Well now, I'll pop along and leave you to it

'YOU'VE NOT GOT A MISSIN' WILL YOU'D LIKE US TO
LOOK FOR, HAVE YOU?' ASKED WILLIAM.

and hope to see the place looking a lot better when I return.'

She trotted back to the house and, peering through the bushes, they saw her setting off with a large shopping basket and making her way down the road.

'*Well!*' said William. '*Weedin'!*' Fancy that! *Weedin'!* It's a s'prise to me there's a single weed left in the world after all those we've pulled up.'

As he looked around, the faces of groundsel, toadflax, nettles, mare's tails and dandelions seemed to leer at him in malicious triumph from among the plants.

'Well, there is,' said Ginger, 'an' I s'pose we'd better start on 'em.'

Half-heartedly William picked a dandelion and laid it in the gardening basket. Then he straightened himself and looked about him again.

'Wonder where that right of way is,' he said.

'It's *weedin'* we've got to do,' Ginger reminded him sternly. 'She was jolly good to us, givin' us all those cakes an' orange squash.'

'Yes, I know,' said William. 'That's what makes me think I'd rather do somethin' more int'resting for her than jus' pullin' up weeds. Anyone could pull up weeds. A *child* could do it. I'd like to do something for her that's got a bit more *adventure* in it. Anyway, you can do *anythin'* for a bob-a-job. Getting back a right of way's as good a bob-a-job as weedin' an' it's a jolly sight more int'restin'.' His eyes went to a little wooden gate at the bottom of the garden. 'I bet that's where it is.'

'We'd better leave it alone, William,' said Ginger. He bent down to remove a piece of groundsel and started back with a yell. 'Gosh! I've been half murdered by a nettle. I wasn't anywhere near it. It jus' sprang out at me. They ought to pay us *danger* money, weedin' with all these nettles . . . Anyway,' resignedly, 'we've got to do weedin' same as she said – after all those cakes.'

But William was already on his way towards the little wooden gate.

'I'm only goin' to have a sort of *look*,' he said. 'I'm not goin' to *do* anythin'. Not unless there's somethin' to *do*, I mean. Well, I mean, it'd be a jolly sight more useful to her to get that right of way fixed than jus' to have a few weeds pulled up. I mean, she was jolly good to us. Gosh! I can still taste that cream bun. I keep tellin' you, I'd like to *do* somethin' for her. I don't call pullin' up weeds *doin'* anythin'. Well, they die nat'ral same as everythin' else if you leave them long enough. Well, it's news to *me* if they don't, so it jus' seems a waste of time pullin' 'em up. If people had any sense they'd jus' wait for 'em to die nat'ral . . . An' I keep tellin' you, I'm only goin' to *look*. You needn't come if you don't want to.'

But Ginger had laid down his trowel and was following William through the little gate.

The gate led to a small spinney of trees at the foot of the

garden of the adjoining house. The spinney had evidently
been left in the same state as when it had formed the boundary
of the original field. The ground beneath the trees was over-
grown with brambles and rough grass, but the path that
formed the right of way was plain to see, winding among the
trees and bushes to the gate at the further end.

'Well, you've *looked*, William,' said Ginger nervously.
'Come on! Let's go back to weedin'.'

'I'm jus' goin' to walk along to the end of the path,' said
William. 'Jus' to make sure it's all right for her. Jus'— *Ow!*'
His arms waved wildly in the air as he fell headlong over a
piece of string that had been fixed across the path beneath the
undergrowth. And that was not all. By some complicated
mechanism the string was connected with a bucket of water
perched on the branches of a tree that stretched out over the
path and its contents descended on to the ground perilously
near William, splashing his entire person. Almost before he
realised what had happened, two boys leapt out from the
cover of a neighbouring holly bush. One was fair with colour-
less eyelashes and projecting teeth. The other was dark with a
long thin pointed nose. Both were grinning derisively.

'Yah! That got you!' said the dark one, dancing about with
glee. 'That got you, all right! That *got* you!'

'*That'll* teach you to come trespassing in other people's
gardens,' shouted the fair one.

William advanced on them bull-like, his neck stretched out,
his face set in lines of ferocity.

'You didn't do it for us,' he said. 'You didn't know we were
comin'. You did it for ole Miss Risborough, didn't you?'

'Yeah, we did,' said the dark one, pointing his long thin
nose at William, 'an' you can tell her so, too.' He turned to his
brother. 'He can tell her so, too, can't he, Hugo?'

'Yeah!' said Hugo, his teeth leaping out in a mocking grimace. 'Yeah, he can, too, Eric . . . An' you can tell her the next

time she comes we're goin' to fix up a meat chopper and see
if we can kill the old girl. And now you can clear off double
quick before we set the police on you for trespassing.'

He put out a hand to push William, and at once William
sprang to the attack. The battle was short and fierce but the
victory was never for a moment in doubt. William was a good
fighter and Ginger an able second, and by the end of three or
four minutes Eric and Hugo were fleeing across the lawn,
closely pursued by their foes. They rushed in at the front door,
slamming it in William's face. Without a moment's hesitation
William and Ginger ran round to the back door, entering it
before the others could reach it. Another battle, also short and
fierce, took place in the hall.

Howling with pain and fury, Eric and Hugo plunged
upstairs. Forgetful of everything but the lust for battle,
William and Ginger plunged upstairs after them. The brothers

'THAT'LL TEACH YOU TO COME TRESPASSING INTO OTHER
PEOPLE'S GARDENS,' SHOUTED THE FAIR BOY.

dashed into a room at the top of the stairs and slammed the
door. The key was on the outside of the door. Instinctively,
and without stopping to think, William turned the key in the
lock.

'Got 'em!' he panted.

From inside the room came the sound of angry shouts and
hammering on the door.

'*Got* 'em!' said William again triumphantly.

'Yes,' said Ginger, 'an' what are we goin' to do about it?'

'What d'you mean, do about it?' said William. He was
flushed with victory, jubilant with the thrill of battle. 'It was a
jolly good fight an' we've got 'em beat an' locked up.'

'Yes,' said Ginger, ''an we're in somebody's else's house

that we don't know an' that we've got no business to be in an'
what's goin' to happen if their father or mother comes home,
that's what *I* want to know.'

William was silent for a moment as the glow of triumph
gradually faded into the cold hard light of reality.

'Well, it's been a nice change from weedin', anyway,' he
said a little lamely.

'Yes, but what are we goin' to *do*?' persisted Ginger.

The tornado of shouts and knocking had died away. There
was an ominous silence behind the locked door, broken by
furtive whispers.

'P'r'aps we'd better let 'em out,' said William.

'Yes, an' start another fight,' said Ginger, 'an' like as not
their mother or father'll come back in the middle of it an'
*then* what'll we say?'

'Oh, I bet I'll think up somethin' to say,' said William airily.

'Yes, an' I bet they'll think up somethin' to *do*,' said
Ginger.

'Well, p'r'aps we'd better go,' agreed William regretfully
as the cold hard light of reality grew colder and harder. 'It was
a jolly good fight an' we've got 'em beat an' locked up an' I
bet we've taught 'em a lesson about messin' up that right of
way.'

'I bet we haven't,' said Ginger, showing a greater knowl-
edge of human nature than his friend. 'I bet we've only made
'em worse. They said they were goin' to kill her next time.'

'Oh, all right,' said William. 'Let's go, then.'

They made their way downstairs and out of the back door,
but before they had taken more than half a dozen steps, a
heavy tile whizzed past William's head, missing it by a frac-
tion of an inch. He looked up to see Eric leaning out of an
open window holding another tile poised for action.

'There's a bit stack of tiles up here,' he yelled, 'that my
dad's got to put in a new fireplace an' you're jolly well goin'

to get 'em all if you try to escape. We're goin' to keep you here till my dad comes home an' then – Gosh! won't he wallop you?'

Another tile whizzed by and William and Ginger dodged hastily back into the doorway for safety.

'Let's try the front,' said William tersely.

But it seemed that the room in which William and Ginger had imprisoned the brothers ran the whole length of the house. Before they had taken two steps out of the front door another tile shot by, grazing William's ear, and they glanced up to see Hugo leaning out of the window, his teeth performing, as it seemed, a dance of triumph while he brandished another tile.

Instinctively William and Ginger dodged back again into the house.

'Let's try the windows,' said William.

But the windows, too, were commanded by the besieged, who had turned so unexpectedly into the besiegers. Heavy tiles whizzed by them on each attempt at escape and after each attempt they dodged back hastily into safety – a safety that seemed to grow more precarious each moment.

'It's worse than those massacre things that happened in hist'ry,' said Ginger, staunching a wound on his forehead with a bedraggled handkerchief. 'Gosh! Stung at by nettles an' hit at by tiles! I bet no one in hist'ry ever had both the same mornin'.'

William was considering the situation with a thoughtful frown.

'We ought to try one of those war escapes,' he said. 'They did it so I don't see why we shouldn't. They dug tunnels. They dug tunnels from where they were imprisoned to outside of it. If we could dig a tunnel from inside the house to ole Miss Risborough's garden . . .'

'How?' challenged Ginger. 'Kin'ly tell me how to dig a

tunnel through people's floor-boards comin' out into other people's gardens. You *tell* me.'

'Oh, shut up!' said William testily. 'There were other ways . . . Some of 'em got out in a wooden horse.'

'All right,' said Ginger, 'find a wooden horse that's big enough for both of us an' then who's goin' to push it, anyway?'

'All right, all *right*,' snapped William. 'If you're goin' to go on an' on makin' objections we're never goin' to get out at all.'

'No, an' I don't think we ever are,' said Ginger gloomily.

'*Tell* you what,' said William suddenly. 'Let's find a little window somewhere where they won't notice an' creep out of that. There might be one in a cupboard somewhere . . . '

He opened a large cupboard that ran beneath the stairs and began to burrow about among the contents. Exultant yells sounded from above.

'Yah! Who thought they were so clever? Yah!'

'Wait till Dad comes home. *He'll* teach you. He ought to be here any minute now, too.'

'You won't find a window there,' said Ginger impatiently.

'P'r'aps not,' said William, interested, despite the urgency of the situation, in the assortment of junk that filled the dark recesses of the cupboard. 'I say! There's a jolly funny thing here.' He dragged out a large copper preserving pan. 'Gosh! I b'lieve it's a sort of saucepan. I bet you could roast an ox whole in it.'

'You *couldn't*,' said Ginger. 'Anyway, we've got no time for roasting oxes even if we could.'

William set the preserving pan down in the hall.

'Yes, it *is* jus' a sort of saucepan. When first I saw it underneath all those other things in the dark it looked smashing. It looked like a sort of giant's helmet. It—' He stopped short and a light dawned slowly over his countenance. 'I say, *Ginger*! I've got an idea.'

'What?' said Ginger a little apprehensively.

'We could *use* it for a giant's helmet. I bet we could get both our heads in it. Gosh! We could get away easy in it. Their old tiles couldn't touch us in it an' it'd be jolly good sucks to them.'

'It'd be a tight squeeze,' said Ginger, looking doubtfully at the pan.

But William's optimism was proof against that objection. He saw his plan already in the rosy light of fulfilment.

'That doesn't matter,' he said. 'Gosh, it's a *wizard* plan. It's jus' like one of those war escapes. I bet it's as good as that wooden horse thing . . . Come on. I'll put my head in first an' then you put yours in.'

It was, as Ginger had said, a tight squeeze, but at last the two heads were safely enclosed in the copper pan and, cautiously, warily, the prisoners felt their way to the back door. Their exit was the signal for a shower of tiles that fell on the pan with no worse effect than a jarring and shaking of the enclosed heads.

'Gosh!' said William. 'That nearly drove my teeth right out through the top of my head.'

But the sound of the breaking tiles and the yells of anger and disappointment from the window above amply compensated for any little inconvenience they might be undergoing, and they chuckled gleefully as they made their journey through the trees that bordered the right of way to the gate that led into Miss Risborough's garden.

'Well, thank goodness we can take it off now,' said William, his voice sounding muffled and resonant inside the copper cavern. Determinedly they set to work to dislodge the pan. With equal determination, as it seemed, the pan set to work not to be dislodged. The rim of the pan was narrower than its body and, though the body could embrace the two heads, the rim refused to do so. They pulled and pushed and wriggled and wrestled. The pan remained immovable. They tried to knock it off against a tree, to rub it off against the fence, to ease it off against a bush ... and still the pan remained immovable.

It is a known fact that prisoners in a confined space are apt to get on each other's nerves, and William and Ginger were no exceptions to the rule.

'I wish you'd keep your ole face to yourself,' said William irritably, ''stead of diggin' it into mine ... Look *out*! You nearly broke my neck then.'

His voice echoed in a strange sepulchral manner round the interior of the copper pan.

'Look out yourself,' said Ginger. 'You've nearly tore my ear off.'

'Well, keep your head out of the *way*.'

'Keep *yours*.'

An attempt at a scuffle brought them heavily to the ground. 'Might as well have a bit of a rest,' said William. 'It might come off better if we'd had a bit of a rest.'

'It couldn't come off worse,' said Ginger.

They sat for some moments in silence. But it was not a peaceful silence. The atmosphere inside the pan was far from peaceful. It was full of pantings and puffings and wrigglings and twitchings and jerkings. William broke the silence. His natural optimism was failing him and darker aspects of the situation came crowding in on his mind.

'S'pose we've got to go about like this till we're old men ... ' he said in a hollow voice.

'With long white beards,' said Ginger, taking a faint unwilling interest in the picture thus called up. 'You can't shave in a saucepan.'

'It's goin' to be jolly difficult to eat in a saucepan,' said William. 'Gosh! I'm beginning to wish I'd never found the thing. I'd sooner be murdered by tiles then starved to death in a saucepan.'

'I wish you'd stop blowin' in my face when you talk.'

'An' I wish you'd stop mooin' in mine when you do.'

'P'r'aps they'll manage to smash it up.'

'Yes, an' what's going to happen to our faces while they do? I don't want to go about without a face for the rest of my life.'

'You'd look a jolly sight better without it,' said Ginger, with a chuckle that sounded like a succession of cannon shots.

Another scuffle precipitated them on to their backs and it took some time to regain a sitting posture.

'An' I bet we get in a row for pinchin' the saucepan,' said Ginger.

'They can't do much to you in a saucepan,' said William. He gave a deep sigh that whistled round the pan like a gust of wind. 'Anyway we prob'ly won't live long. I never heard of anyone livin' long in a saucepan. I'd've made my will again if I'd known . . . I made a new one last week but I forgot to leave my c'lection of insects to the British Museum.'

'I bet we don't even get that bob for the job,' said Ginger. 'We've not done any weedin'.'

'Well, let's have another shot at it now.'

With difficulty they scrambled to their feet and began once more the long unequal struggle.

'You jus' aren't *tryin'* to make your head go small,' said William in a tone of exasperation as he pushed and pulled unavailingly. 'You're jus' keepin' it as big as you can.'

'I like that!' said Ginger heatedly. 'I could get mine out easy if you wouldn't keep pushin' yours in front of it.'

Suddenly Miss Risborough's voice floated gently over the garden.

'Boys! . . . Where are you, boys?'

'Come on,' muttered William. 'We'd better go to her.'

Unsteadily the strange four-legged apparition, crowned by the copper pan, made its slow progress over the lawn – a

UNSTEADILY THE FOUR-LEGGED APPARITION MADE ITS
SLOW PROGRESS OVER THE LAWN.

progress still further hampered by a sudden attempt at flight
on Ginger's part.

The two were strung up to meet anger, reproaches,
demands for explanations ... but all they heard was a gay
little laugh as Miss Risborough, easing and manoeuvring the
preserving pan, gently detached it from their heads.

They stood there, blinking, drawing deep breaths.

'What a charming and amusing way of bringing it back to
me, boys!' she said. 'You've got quite a sense of humour ...'
They gaped at her in astonishment and she went on, 'Actually

'd quite forgotten that I'd told you about that particular worry
f mine. Somehow I thought it was my right of way worry I'd
old you about, but I've got a most unreliable memory.' She
azed fondly down at the pan that lay on the grass at her feet.
I'm *so* glad to get it back. As I must have told you, those
readful boys' mother borrowed it then simply *denied* that
he'd got it or even seen it . . . Perhaps she'd forgotten or just
ost it . . . but, anyway, it isn't really mine. It belongs to my
ister and she's coming to collect it tomorrow and I was terri-
ied of having to tell her that I hadn't got it. It was so good of
ou to bring it back for me, boys. I don't know how you found
t and perhaps I'd better not ask, but I'm *most* grateful.'

'Oh!' said William, collecting his scattered forces as best
e could. 'Well, axshully we sort of set out to get that right of
vay thing put right . . .'

'Oh, that!' said the old lady. 'That's quite all right now. I
net Mrs Jones in the village and happened to tell her about it
nd she said I could always go through her garden to the bus
top and that's an even shorter cut than the other.'

William was rubbing his neck, which still felt disjointed by
ts sojourn in the copper pan.

''Fraid we've not done much weedin',' he said.

'That doesn't really matter,' said the old lady. 'I've come to
he conclusion that one must just *resign* oneself to weeds.
You've taken a lot of trouble, I'm sure, getting back my pre-
erving pan. Funny that I quite forgot I'd told you about it, but
oth those worries have been preying on my mind, so no
vonder I get them mixed. It's so nice to have them both
leared up the same day . . . Well, I think you've done a very
;ood hour's work, boys. Where are your cards? . . . Now
vhat shall I put? "Recovering missing preserving pan"
ounds so odd, doesn't it? I think I'll put "General helpful-
less". That sounds better, doesn't it? And here are your
hillings and thank you so much.'

Dazedly they took their leave of her and made their way
back to the road.

'Gosh!' said Ginger. 'I never thought I'd get out of that
saucepan alive.'

But William's thoughts lingered over the adventure. Bathed
in the glamour of the past, it was already assuming heroic
proportions in his mind. He walked with a dare-devil air. He
kicked a stone from one side of the road to the other with a
nonchalant swagger.

'It was a jolly good fight,' he said, 'an' we beat 'em an'
locked 'em up an' got her saucepan back an' fixed up her
right o' way—'

'*We* didn't,' Ginger reminded him.

'Oh, well, we nearly did. I bet we did really. I bet those two
wouldn't have dared to do anythin' more to her after that.' He
chuckled. 'I wonder if they're still locked up in that room. I'd
like to go back an' see.'

'Well, you can't,' said Ginger. 'We couldn't go back without that sauceapan an' I bet old Miss Risborough wouldn't
lend it us jus' to keep tiles off.'

'What'll we do, then?'

'We'll do another bob-a-job,' said Ginger. 'There's time to
do another.'

'Not weedin',' stipulated William.

'No, not weedin',' agreed Ginger.

Frankie Parker passed them on his bicycle. He waved his
bob-a-job book exultantly.

'I've had a smashing time,' he called. 'I've cleaned windows and painted a gate. The gate was super.'

'That's what we'll do,' said William. 'We'll paint a gate.
Paintin' anything gen'rally turns out excitin'.'

'An' cleanin' a window'd be next best,' said Ginger.

'Yes,' said William. 'I once did one at home, but a bit got
broke off an' the ladder went through the rest an' I got a lot o

water over me an' they wouldn't let me go on with it. I bet I could manage it all right now. Come on. Let's find a house.'

They walked down the road, examining each house as they passed it.

'That one's got dirty windows,' said Ginger at last.

'Yes,' said William, '*an*' its gate wants paintin'. Come on!'

A tall thin woman with a smudge of flour down her overall opened the door to them.

'We've come to paint your gate,' said William brusquely.

She stared at him.

'Come to – *what*?' she said.

'Or clean your windows,' said William hastily.

'Bob-a-job,' said Ginger.

Her expression relaxed. She beamed a welcome.

'Oh, yes,' she said. 'Come in. This way.'

'Axshully we'd rather do the gate than the windows,' said William. 'We're better at gates.'

The woman did not seem to hear. She took them through the house to the back garden and pointed out a patch of weed-infested ground enclosed by a small box-edging.

'It's my herb garden,' she said, 'and I want all those weeds taken up.'

There was a stricken look on William's face.

'We'll do the gate first,' he said desperately.

'But, I don't *want* the gate done.'

'We'll start with the windows, then.'

'I don't want the windows done. I want my herb bed weeded.'

'Well, listen,' said William hoarsely. 'Haven't you any missing wills you'd like us to find for you or clues to track for you or – or we can get saucepans back an' rights of ways an' – an'—'

'Don't be silly,' said the woman. 'Just set to work on the herb garden.'

'We've never *done* a herb garden,' pleaded William.

'It's just like any other sort of garden,' said the woman impatiently. 'Now, don't waste any more time. And work thoroughly and conscientiously.'

She went indoors. They stood gazing down gloomily at the herb garden.

'Haunted by weeds,' said William bitterly, 'that's what we are. Jus' *haunted* by 'em. Everything we try 'n' do turns into weeds.'

'The last one didn't,' said Ginger. 'It turned out of 'em pretty quick.'

William gave his short sarcastic laugh.

'I bet this one won't,' he said.

'Well, come on,' said Ginger. 'We'll have to do it.'

'What *are* herbs?' said William with a faint flicker of interest.

'Some sort of flower, I s'pose,' said Ginger vaguely. 'I 'spect we'll come across them as we go along. Come on, let's do it. Thoroughly an' conscientiously, same as she said.'

'All right,' said William. He spoke in the tone of one who yields to a dark and inexorable fate. 'All right, I s'pose we'll have to. There's different sorts of weeds growin' here, anyway, an' that'll be a bit of a change.'

Silently, gloomily, thoroughly, conscientiously, they went to work, pulling up handfuls of groundsel, dandelions, goosegrass, bindweed, mint, parsley, thyme, marjoram and chives . . .

# Chapter 7

# William and the Wedding Anniversary

It was Ethel's idea to make an Occasion of her parents' wedding anniversary. In previous years Mr Brown had either forgotten the date altogether or had – a little shamefacedly – brought home for his wife a bunch of flowers that bore all the marks of rush-hour travel. But this year, said Ethel, they must do the thing properly.

'The darlings must have a party,' she said. 'A real party. And they mustn't have any of the worry of the preparations. We'll see to everything.'

She and Robert were holding a private meeting in Robert's bedroom to discuss the arrangements. William had not been invited to it, but, realising that something unusual was afoot, he had slipped into the room after them and taken his position tailor-fashion on the hearthrug.

'I've got as much right as you have,' he said when challenged. 'It's as much my father an' mother's wedding thing as it is your father an' mother's wedding thing . . . Well, people'll think it jolly funny if I don't help with it. It'll seem sort of *fishy*. Gosh!' – with his short sarcastic laugh – 'they'll begin to think there's somethin' wrong with me.'

'They won't begin to think anything of the sort,' said Ethel. 'They've known it for long enough.'

William's indignation increased.

'Let *me* tell *you*—' he began, but Robert silenced him by a curt:

'All right. You can stay as long as you keep quiet.'

Robert sat at his writing-desk, wearing a business-like air and a purposeful frown, his pencil poised over a writing-pad. Ethel reclined at ease in the dilapidated wicker arm-chair that Robert had recently salvaged from the loft in order to transform his bedroom into a bed-sitting room.

'The main thing is to get it thoroughly organised from the beginning,' said Robert. There were times when Robert suspected that he possessed organising abilities which, properly directed, might sway the fate of nations. 'It's the loose ends that cause trouble. The secret of the whole thing is to leave no loose ends that can possibly cause trouble later.'

'Yes,' agreed Ethel absently.

She had discovered that the double reflection of the dressing-table mirror and the shaving mirror over the hand basin gave her a perfect view of her profile and she was studying it with interest.

William watched sombrely from the hearthrug.

'I think we should decide first of all the form the entertainment is to take,' said Robert with a magisterial air.

Ethel tore herself from the study of her profile.

'Dancing, of course,' she said.

'Dancing?' echoed William in a tone of surprised disgust. 'Gosh! I bet I could think of somethin' better than dancin'. Listen! I could do some conjurin' tricks for you. I've got some jolly good conjurin' tricks. I've got one where I turn a—'

'Shut up!' said Robert.

'Or an animal show,' persisted William. 'Listen, I could get up a jolly good animal show. There's Jumble an' my stag beetle to start with an' Frankie Parker's got a white rat that does tricks that he wants to sell an' there's Ginger's cat an' Henry's tortoise an' Douglas's rabbit. I could get up a *smashin'* animal show with those an' I bet people'd like it better than a lot of ole dancin'.'

'We don't *want* an animal show,' said Robert crushingly, 'so you can shut up.'

'Well, listen,' said William, uncrushed. 'If you don't want an animal show or conjuring tricks, what about a play? I've written a play about crim'nals an' a ghost that's jolly good an' Ginger an' Douglas an' Henry an' me'll act it for you an' if you don't want a play about crim'nals an' a ghost I can write one about someone travellin' in space an' gettin' stuck on a comet an'—'

'Will you shut up!' said Robert, half-rising from his chair.

'Oh, all right,' said William, relaxing despondently on to his hearthrug. 'If you don't want a decent party I can't help it. I bet you'll wish you'd listened to me when it's all over. I bet they'll feel so fed up when they find it's only dancin' that they'll all go home soon as they get here. I know I would. I know I'd go home if I got to a party an' found it was only dancin'. That ole dancin' class I go to – well, it's jus' mental torcher.'

'Strange as it may seem to you,' said Ethel, 'we and our friends enjoy dancing.'

'And one more word from you—' added Robert darkly.

'Oh, all right,' said William. 'Only don't blame me when it's all over an' everybody's sayin' what a rotten time they've had.'

'No, we won't,' said Ethel. 'And now about the guests . . . Who shall we invite, Robert?'

'Well, I'd like Jameson and Hector and perhaps Ronald . . . '

'And Rowena,' suggested Ethel kindly.

'Well – er – yes, I'd like Rowena,' said Robert a little self-consciously, 'and perhaps Peggy and Marion. And what about you? Jimmy Moore?'

'Well, yes,' said Ethel. 'Jimmy and Charles and Dorita and perhaps Richard . . . '

Robert's pencil moved swiftly over the paper as the list of names grew. Gordon Franklin . . . Dolly Clavis . . . Sheila Barron . . .

'Here!' interposed William at last on a squeak of indignation. 'What about me?'

'What d'you mean, what about you?' said Robert.

'Well, what about the ones I'm goin' to invite? I want Ginger an' Henry an' Douglas, anyway.'

'This isn't a children's party,' said Ethel.

'Well, if *you're* goin' to invite people, I don't see why I shouldn't,' said William with spirit. 'I keep tellin' you it's as much my mother an' father's wedding thing as it is your mother an' father's wedding thing. An' I bet my friends could make a party a jolly sight more excitin' than yours could. Well, I *know* they could. Gosh, that party of Ginger's last Christmas was *wizard*. Ginger an' me made up a new game for it that started with two people havin' a duel an' ended with everyone else joinin' in. Listen! I'll 'splain about this new game that Ginger an' me made up an' I bet if you'd let Ginger an' me get it started for you it'd turn out the most excitin' party you've ever had.'

'I've no doubt it would,' said Ethel. 'That's exactly what we're afraid of.'

'But *listen*—' began William again.

'You can have one guest and no more,' said Robert in a tone of finality.

For a moment William's sense of outrage deprived him of speech, then speech returned.

'*One?* Me only have *one* an' you havin' hundreds an' hundreds! Gosh! You're havin' everyone anyone ever heard of an' – Gosh! me only *one*!'

'We've already told you this isn't a children's party,' said

Robert, 'and we've had quite enough of your cheek, so you can clear out.'

'All right,' said William. 'I don't want to stay here anyway. I don't want to go on wastin' my time tryin' to help people that don't want to be helped an' that don't know what's an excitin' party an' what isn't. If I can't have more 'n one I won't have any.' He rose with dignity from his seat on the hearthrug. 'An' I wouldn't help you now, not if – not if you came on your bended knees beggin' me to.'

He withdrew from the room, much impressed by his parting speech.

'Huh!' he said to himself, as he slid down the banisters and landed in a heap at the bottom of the stairs. 'I bet they're feelin' small.'

But he was mistaken. Robert and Ethel were not feeling small. Robert was looking at his list of guests as if struck by a sudden doubt.

'Perhaps they're a bit *young*,' he was saying. 'For the parents, I mean.'

'Oh, no, they love young people,' said Ethel carelessly. 'They'll adore it.'

William had whistled for Jumble and, with Jumble at his heels, was wandering slowly down the road, hands plunged into his pockets, brows drawn into a thoughtful frown . . . It was going to be a rotten party. Gosh! If they'd only let him help! His thoughts went to the parties in which he and the other Outlaws had turned their respective houses into bedlam for a brief and glorious hour.

'Dancin'!' he muttered disgustedly. 'Jus' dancin'!'

Even the sight of Jumble worrying a piece of dead wood in the ditch, throwing it into the air, shaking it in his mouth, growling at it threateningly, failed to raise his spirits.

So absorbed was he in his grievances that he did not notice

he was passing the Parkers' gate and that Frankie Parker was emerging from it till Frankie accosted him with a loud, 'Hi, William!'

'Hello,' answered William morosely.

Then he noticed that Frankie was holding something concealed in his hands. His interest rose and curiosity got the better of his dejection.

'What's that?' he said.

Frankie opened his hands, revealing a sleek white form.

'It's that white rat I told you about,' he said. 'It's a *wizard* rat an' I'm sellin' it for sixpence. It's a *bargain*, William. You won't get another white rat like this for sixpence, not all the rest of your life. Not if you went all over the world, you wouldn't.'

William's interest rose higher and something of his animation returned.

'You said it did tricks,' he said.

'Yes, it does.'

'It's not doin' any now.'

'It's shy,' explained Frankie. 'It'll do them when it comes out of bein' shy. It's a *smashing* rat, William. I bet you'd have to pay *pounds* for a rat like this in a shop. An' it's only sixpence.'

'Well, that's all the money I've got,' said William. 'I've only got sixpence.'

'Well, you've *got* sixpence,' urged Frankie, 'so it's all right. You can buy it all right if you've *got* sixpence. Gosh! I bet you'll be sorry all the rest of your life if you don't buy it. Victor Jameson wants to buy it but I thought I'd give you first chance. I bet there isn't a boy in the whole world wouldn't want to buy it, if he got first chance. Gosh, you're lucky to have first chance.'

Frankie was a good salesman and, before he quite knew what he was doing, William had handed over his sixpence and taken the white rat in exchange.

'IT'S NOT DOIN' ANY TRICKS,' SAID WILLIAM, GAZING
CRITICALLY AT HIS PURCHASE.

'It's called Edgar after my father,' said Frankie, 'and it's the
most intelligent rat I've ever had.'

Edgar lay on William's palm, gazing around with a super-
cilious air.

Jumble stood on his hind legs, sniffed the newcomer, then
walked off casually to investigate the ditch. Jumble's lack of
interest in Edgar increased William's doubts.

'It's still not doin' tricks,' he said, gazing critically at his
purchase.

'I told you it's shy,' said Frankie. 'Jus' wait till it comes out
of bein' shy . . . Well, I've got to be off now. I've got to do
some errands for my aunt.'

With that he set off briskly down the road.

Edgar turned out to be an ancient lethargic rat who dozed
away his time either in William's pocket or in the straw-lined
box prepared for it by William in the garage – and consumed
unlimited quantities of household scraps.

Frankie, taxed with the failure of his late pet to make
good his promises, was outraged and incredulous. He paid

Edgar a visit and interpreted each sleepy movement as a 'trick'.

'Look, William. He's doing "Eyes Right" like a soldier . . . Now he's doing "Eyes Left" . . . Now he's wrinkling up his nose like a rabbit . . . An' look at him *now*, William. He's standing on his hind legs . . . Yes, I know I'm holding his front legs. Well, nat'rally I've got to hold his front legs for him to stand on his hind ones . . . *Now* look at him, William. He's dancing . . . Yes, I know I'm helping him a little, but I'm only being same as his partner. Well, yumans have to have partners holding them and helping them to dance, don't they? So it's a jolly clever trick, dancing like a yuman. I bet not many rats can dance like yumans . . . An' look!' He drew from his pocket a small unrecognisable object covered with fluff, which he carefully detached from it. 'It's a piece of toffee an' he's jolly fond of toffee. Now look!' He held the toffee just out of Edgar's reach. 'Don't eat it, Edgar. There's an atom bomb inside it . . . Look! He's not eating it . . . It's all right now, Edgar. You can eat it. There isn't an atom bomb inside it now . . . There! . . . Did you see him eat it?'

'Well, you practic'ly shoved it in his mouth,' said William, 'an' you held it so far away he couldn't have got it before that, anyway.'

'Gosh! He could 've got it if he'd wanted to,' said Frankie indignantly. 'That was his trick, not doin'. A jolly clever trick, too.'

Frankie was no charlatan. He honestly saw Edgar as a super rat, a wonder rat, a miracle rat. He had sold him only because his other pets – a hedgehog, a tortoise, a guinea pig and a hamster (all of which he considered to be gifted with supreme intelligence) took so much time and food that he had reluctantly decided to part with Edgar.

Something of his enthusiasm communicated itself to

William and gradually he began to look on Edgar's very inertness as a mark of wisdom and intellect. And Jumble's lack of interest in the new pet simplified the situation. More than one of the white rats that William had previously owned had fallen a victim to Jumble's interest.

He had completely forgotten the party that was to celebrate his parents' wedding anniversary till he overheard Robert and Ethel discussing the gift – a picnic basket – that they intended to present to them during the course of the party. Then, for the first time, the disturbing thought struck William. He, too, should have some gift to offer . . .

He examined the shops of the neighbourhood, extending the search as far as Marleigh, where he discovered a glass ash-tray of virulent colour and design marked sixpence. He gazed at it in wistful admiration. It was more striking in every way, he considered, than a picnic basket. It was colourful, handsome and unusual – a worthy memento of a great occasion. And it was only sixpence. His spirits rose . . . then sank, as he remembered that he did not possess sixpence; he had spent his last sixpence on Edgar. He returned home, transferred Edgar from box to his pocket, then went round to Frankie Parker's, offering to re-sell his pet for the sixpence he had paid for it.

But Frankie, intent on organising a wrestling match between his guinea pig and hamster, had no interest to spare for Edgar.

'The ole rat?' he said briefly. 'No, thanks.'

William then proceeded to offer Edgar for sale publicly and privately among his friends, but the few who possessed the sum of sixpence had other plans for it. In any case they didn't want a white rat. Edgar, exposed in the open market, still failed to find a buyer.

'Gosh! It looks old, doesn't it?'

'Looks bats to me.'

William rose hotly in defence of his pet, but without avail.

'Well, he may *be* intell'gent,' said Johnny Smith, who had been offered Edgar at the reduced price of fivepence three farthings. 'All I say is he doesn't *look* it.'

It was not till the day before the party was to take place that the idea occurred to William of offering Edgar to his parents as a gift. After all, he represented sixpence in hard cash, and William had become so accustomed to his bland inoffensive presence that he had begun to conceive a deep affection for him – an affection that, he felt, must be shared by anyone who came to know him. He's better than those budge birds, anyway, he ruminated. He stays quiet and doesn't make a fool of himself tryin' to talk. But he realised that the idea would take a little leading up to, that to present his father with a white rat in cold blood would be to court rebuff and possibly disaster. Mr Brown would not at first appreciate the unique advantages of Edgar as a pet. He might even view the gesture in the light of an insult.

He approached his father warily that evening as he sat in his arm-chair by the fire reading the paper.

'I say, Dad—' he began.

Mr Brown grunted.

'You know, white rats make jolly good pets,' said William.

Mr Brown grunted again.

'I mean they're quiet,' went on William, elaborating his theme. 'They don't try to talk, I mean, same as those budge birds . . . Well, I mean, you like quiet, don't you?'

'I do, my boy,' said Mr Brown meaningly.

'Well, I b'lieve you'd *like* a white rat. A quiet one, I mean. One that could do quiet sort of tricks. Well, Jumble likes it an' *he's* got a bit of sense. Well, he doesn't *not* like it, I mean. He jus' doesn't take any notice of it . . . but I bet you'd like it. It'd be comp'ny. It stays quiet in your pocket for hours an' hours. You could take it along with you anywhere – to – to golf or the office or anywhere an' – an' – well, it'd be comp'ny.'

He paused. Mr Brown had lost interest in the subject and returned to his paper. But William now considered that the ground had been sufficiently prepared for the final assault.

'I say, Dad—' he began again.

Mr Brown's answering grunt suggested patience strained almost to breaking point.

'I say, Dad, I've been sort of wondering what you'd like for your present. For this wedding thing party you're havin' tomorrow. I was wonderin' what you'd like for it an' I was jus' sort of wonderin' if you'd like a—'

He stopped. Mr Brown had lowered his paper abruptly. His expression was not encouraging. Mr Brown had that morning received a bill from his builders that included a window broken by William, a fence broken by William, a gate broken by William, and a greenhouse roof broken by William. Punishment had been meted out on each separate occasion, but the sum total was such as to cause Mr Brown to regard his son with a far from indulgent eye. Moreover the festivities arranged for his wedding anniversary tomorrow failed to rouse his enthusiasm. Not wishing to show himself churlish and ungrateful, he was trying gallantly to conceal his feelings, but the prospect of seeing his home turned upside down for a young people's party – when he would rather have spent the evening by the fire alone with his wife or with some old crony – weighed down his spirit . . . and his general feeling of irritation found outlet in his voice as he said,

'One human civilised action from you, my boy, would be all I could wish for in the way of a present – but that is, I'm afraid, too much to hope for.'

'Oh,' said William blankly.

Mr Brown returned to his newspaper and William went out into the garden to consider the situation. He didn't know what 'one human civilised action' meant, but he was pretty sure it didn't mean a white rat. There remained the ash-tray, but, first of all, he must somehow or other find the sum of sixpence. He was still standing there, frowning deeply, trying to grapple with the problem that confronted him, when Mrs Brown's voice roused him from his reverie.

'Bedtime, William!' she called.

Oh well, thought William with his usual optimism as he turned to go indoors, there was all tomorrow to get the money and buy the present. Just as well that his father hadn't wanted Edgar. He'd have missed him . . .

His optimism still upheld him as he set off after school the next afternoon, with Edgar in his pocket and Jumble at his heels, and made his way along the Marleigh road. He had no very definite plans. He might do an errand for someone or chop firewood for someone or sweep a path for someone . . . and they'd have to give him sixpence for it. Anyway, he trusted to Fate to provide an opening. And Fate did.

His eye fell suddenly on a notice in a shop window: 'BOY WANTED'. He stopped abruptly and stood considering it. Well, he was a boy, all right, and if they wanted a boy it meant they'd be willing to pay for a boy.

'Come on, Jumble,' he said, opening the door.

At the sound of the little tinkling bell, the woman who sat knitting behind the counter looked up with a vague smile. It was a tightly-packed little shop. Groceries, ironmongery, shoes, bottles of sweets, aprons and shopping baskets were stacked on shelves and counter or dangled from the ceiling.

'What can I do for you?' said the woman.

William had assumed his most business-like air.

'There's a notice about a boy in the window,' he said.

'Yes, I believe there is,' said the woman.

'Well, I'm one,' said William simply.

'Yes,' said the woman with another vague smile. She stopped to pick up a stitch and added, 'I see you are.'

'Well, would I do?' said William, dragging Jumble away from a sack of dog biscuits on the floor.

'I really don't know,' said the woman. 'It isn't my shop. It's my sister's and she's out. I'm only staying with her.'

'I s'pose I'd get paid for it,' said William tentatively. 'Bein' a boy, I mean.'

Edgar, attracted by the smell of a slab of cheese on the counter, poked his head out of William's pocket. William gently pushed it back.

'I suppose so,' said the woman. 'I don't know how much, but fair wages, I'm sure. It's for delivering goods, you know. An errand boy.' She paused and added mildly, 'You haven't a lead for your dog, have you?'

'No,' said William, retrieving a bedroom slipper that Jumble was in process of worrying and pushing down Edgar, whose nose had again appeared over the top of William's pocket, quivering in ecstasy at the delicious scent.

'You seem to have your hands full,' said the woman.

'They like shops,' said William. 'They get a bit excited when they get into them.' He grasped Jumble firmly by the collar with one hand and held down Edgar in his pocket with the other as he continued, 'I can't be a reg'lar boy 'cause of school an' things.'

'I thought you looked a bit young for it,' said the woman, 'but I didn't like to say so.'

'I'm not *young*,' said William with a touch of dignity. 'I'm over eleven . . . but what I wanted to know was, could I do a *bit* of bein' a boy? Jus' – well, jus' about sixpennyworth. An' could I do it now 'cause it's rather important?'

The woman's eye roved round the shop and came to rest on a paper bag at the edge of the counter.

'Well, now,' she said, 'it's a funny thing but Miss Gilpin's forgot that bag of biscuits. She put all the other things she bought into her bag but forgot the biscuits.' She rose, carefully insinuating her head between a saucepan and a dustpan. 'My sister's a short woman so they don't worry her but I nearly cut my head open on a garden trowel the other day getting up too quick.' She handed the bag of biscuits to William. 'Suppose you take them round to her. She lives at Hillcrest just up the road with her brother. They only moved in last week. She's sure to give you sixpence for it.'

'Thanks,' said William, his spirits rising.

He set off down the road, turned to find Jumble following him with a rubber boot in his mouth, went back to the shop to restore the rubber boot, then once more set off in search of Hillcrest.

It was a small neat house on the top of the hill. William stood looking at it thoughtfully for a few moments, then walked up to the front door and knocked. Jumble stood beside him, wagging his tail in happy anticipation. Jumble always wagged his tail in happy anticipation when awaiting the opening of a door on which William had knocked. No amount of experience could ever convince him that he would not be a welcome and expected guest.

No one answered the knock. William knocked again. There was still no sound of movement in the house. He walked round to the back door and beat a loud tattoo on it with his knuckles. Still no one answered. But the door stood ajar and, tentatively, curiously, William pushed it open. It revealed an empty tidy kitchen with a glowing boiler fire and a gay woollen rug on the hearth. A chair near the table was piled with paper bags of groceries. Evidently Miss Gilpin had put her purchases there on returning from the shop and then gone out again. William laid the bag of biscuits on the chair with the other things. He'd wait there, he decided, till she came back. He didn't want to miss his sixpence after taking all this trouble.

The sound of a hiss and a snarl startled him and he turned to
see that a black cat had risen from the hearth-rug and was
standing, back arched, fur erect, confronting Jumble. Jumble
enjoyed chasing cats but had never yet solved the problem of
how to deal with a cat that refused to be chased. So he stood –
rigid, growling softly – waiting for his enemy to turn to flight.
The cat, however, had no intention of turning to flight. So the
two stood, frozen and immobile, staring fixedly at each other.
William was just bending down to take Jumble by the collar
and lead him from the scene of danger when something
wholly unexpected happened. Edgar, intoxicated by the smell
of Danish Blue, had shed his usual lethargy. Rakishly, tipsily,
he poked his head again from William's pocket, evaded
William's restraining hand and slid down his legs on to the
floor.

Immediately pandemonium broke out in the kitchen. The
cat leapt after Edgar. Jumble leapt after the cat. Edgar, still
intoxicated by the memories of Danish Blue, raced with
meteor-like swiftness round the room, followed by the cat and
Jumble. Jumble crashed against the chair, overturning it.
Rice, sugar, currants and biscuits fell to the ground and rolled
all over the floor . . . and still the wild pursuit continued.

'Hi!' shouted William desperately. 'Hi! . . . Down, Jumble!
. . . Down, Edgar! . . . Down, cat!'

Suddenly Edgar fled through the half-open door that led
into the hall. The others followed, William just in time to see
Edgar slip into the open door of a cupboard beneath the stairs.
Anxious to secure his pet, William plunged in after him and,
grabbing hold of a hook on the back of the door, slammed it
to. Jumble had slipped in after them. The cat fortunately had
not. Edgar sat up drunkenly in a corner of the cupboard,
combing his whiskers. William secured him, stuffed him into
his pocket and then turned his attention to Jumble, who, finding that his enemy had escaped him, was scratching wildly at

the door, trying to get out. William took him by the collar and held him firmly.

'Gosh!' he panted. 'Let's get out of this quick as we can.'

He pushed the door. It refused to move . . . Gradually, with dawning horror, he realised that it was the sort of door that

'DOWN, JUMBLE!' SHOUTED WILLIAM DESPERATELY.
'DOWN, EDGAR! DOWN, CAT!'

can only be opened from outside. There was no catch or handle of any sort inside it. He was locked into this small dark prison with Edgar and Jumble and with no possibility of escape.

Gone was the chance of earning sixpence. Gone, in all probability, was the chance of attending his parents' wedding anniversary celebrations. But those were the least of his fears. What was to happen when the owners of the house returned

and found the kitchen carpeted by groceries and a strange boy and dog in possession of the cupboard beneath the stairs? He fiddled about with the fastening of the door and found it solidly immovable. He even held Edgar up to it with vague memories of rats in stories who had gnawed their way through solid barriers, but Edgar, after giving the wood an experimental lick and finding that it was not Danish Blue, relapsed into his old inertia and settled down for a doze.

William didn't know how long he had remained in his prison when there came the sound of a woman's footsteps entering the kitchen. They stopped suddenly and a shrill scream rang through the house.

'Good Heavens! What's happened? What on earth's happened?'

Jumble uttered a low growl, but William, intent on putting

off the moment of their discovery as long as possible, held his muzzle tightly in one hand.

'*Tiddles!*' screamed the woman. 'What are you doing up there on top of the dresser, my darling? Oh, dear! Oh, dear! What *has* happened?'

Jumble's bark, strangled by William's restraining hand, floated out from the cupboard.

'Oh, my goodness!' said the woman on an ascending squeak.

Her footsteps approached the cupboard. A muffled snarl from Jumble sent her scurrying back to the kitchen.

Almost immediately there came the sound of more footsteps, and a man's voice exclaimed:

'Good Lord, Agatha! What on earth is all this?'

The woman's voice answered tearfully:

'Oh, Ambrose, I'm so glad you've come. The most dreadful thing has happened.'

'I can see that the most dreadful thing's happened. Sugar and rice and currants and what-not all over the place! But who on earth did it?'

'A lunatic, Ambrose. And he's here in the house.'

'In the house? Where?'

'In the cupboard under the stairs. He's making horrible animal noises.'

'Animal noises?'

'Yes, animal noises . . . Moans and groans . . . Horrible . . . He must have escaped from somewhere . . . I'd been to the shop for the groceries and then I just slipped out to the post to post a letter and when I came back he was *here*. The groceries were flung all over the floor like this – who but a madman, Ambrose, would throw rice and sugar and biscuits all over the floor? – and poor Tiddles was up there on top of the dresser. She must have *sensed* that something evil had come into the house. Then I went into the hall and I heard him in the cupboard under the stairs making horrible animal noises. I heard him move, too. He sounded a large powerfully-built man. Perhaps we'd better send for the police, Ambrose.'

'No, no,' said the man's voice impatiently. 'I'll tackle him. Where did you say he was? In the cupboard under the stairs?'

'Yes . . . Do be careful, Ambrose.'

Footsteps approached the cupboard and stopped outside it. Jumble, in a frenzy of excitement, emitted a series of smothered barks between William's hands.

'There!' said the woman. 'I told you he was making horrible animal noises.'

A deep smothered growl came from the recesses of the cupboard.

'Perhaps he's ill,' said the man. A strangled snarl floated out into the hall. 'He sounds ill.'

'A man who's ill wouldn't throw rice and currants all over the floor, Ambrose. Unless, of course, he's delirious. Perhaps he *is* delirious . . . Oh, Ambrose, let's dial 999.'

'*No*,' said Ambrose. 'Now stand on one side, my dear.' There was a short silence; then the cupboard door was flung open. 'I'm armed, my man. You'd better come quietly . . . '

He stopped short and stood gazing in amazement at the small boy and the dog crouching on the floor in front of him.

As he gazed amazement gave place to anger. That all this worry and upset, all this trepidation and gathering up of his courage should have been caused by one small boy and a mongrel dog! It was outrageous. He would have faced a desperate villain with far less indignation. He caught hold of William's collar and jerked him out into the hall. Jumble followed, wagging his tail in a deprecating, apologetic fashion, aware that he and his master had once again stumbled into trouble. Edgar, who had exhausted his sudden spurt of energy, slept peacefully among the other oddments in William's pocket.

'What do you mean by it?' said the man furiously. He was

HE FLUNG OPEN THE CUPBOARD DOOR AND GAZED IN
AMAZEMENT AT THE SMALL BOY AND DOG.

a large man with flaming red hair and bright blue eyes. 'How *dare* you! . . . I suppose you are responsible for the disgraceful state of the kitchen?'

'Well, in a kind of a way I am,' admitted William breathlessly, 'but it wasn't my fault. Listen! I—'

'Forcing your way into a private house, wrecking the kitchen, trespassing—'

'Frightening the cat,' put in the woman.

'Is this your idea of a joke?' said the man.

'No,' said William, wriggling unavailingly in the vice-like grip. 'No, it jolly well *isn't* my idea of a joke. Listen! I can 'splain it all. I—'

The man gave him a shake that made his teeth rattle.

'Where do you live?'

With a sinking heart William muttered his address.

'Come on, then,' said the man. 'I'll take you there and your father shall hear of your disgraceful conduct. I hope he'll deal with you most severely. Forcing your way into people's houses without so much as a "by your leave" . . . '

'I knocked,' put in William.

'—Flinging groceries all over the floor out of pure devilment, trespassing all over the place, hiding in that cupboard—'

'Frightening the cat,' put in the woman again.

'Heaven only knows what damage you've done to the rest of the house.' He turned to the woman. 'Go up and see what damage he's done to the rest of the house.'

The woman went upstairs. William tried again to explain the situation but each attempt was choked at birth by another fierce shaking from his captor.

'No, he hasn't done any damage upstairs, Ambrose,' said the woman returning.

'Only because he didn't have the chance,' said the man. 'He heard you coming and slipped into that cupboard. Well, we'll see what his father has to say to him, and' – grimly – 'I hope *do* to him. Come along.'

He jerked William out of the hall and through the kitchen. Jumble followed dejectedly, only stopping to retrieve a biscuit from the kitchen floor, crunching and swallowing it in one swift movement. The cat, restored to its old position on the hearthrug, eyed them with an air of sardonic triumph as they passed.

They went down the garden path and along the road towards William's home, William pouring out a confused explanation of his plight. The man received it in stony silence without relaxing his grip.

Finally William's voice died away and the two walked on in silence through the dusk. Apprehension lay like ice at William's heart. He tried to imagine their arrival at his home, their reception by his father, but even William's imagination boggled at the prospect. The guests would all be there. The party would be in full swing. Instead of arriving as an honoured son of the house, bearing his gift and presenting it proudly to his parents, he would be dragged in as a criminal to justice. He tried to imagine his father's and mother's anger . . . the shame of Robert and Ethel . . . the horror of the guests . . . the endless humiliation . . . the stigma that would attach to him for evermore of having publicly disgraced his family on this great occasion. He hung back, dragging his toes in the dust.

'Come on,' snapped the man, ruthlessly jerking him forward once more.

In at the gate . . . up the path to the front door.

'They're prob'ly out,' said William, his voice hoarse with desperation.

'Out!' said the man, raising his hand to the knocker. 'Look at all the lights.'

'They may've left them on by mistake,' pleaded William. 'They may've forgot to turn them off when they went out. They do often forget to turn them off . . . Listen, let's come tomorrow. I promise I'll come with you tomorrow. I know they'll be in tomorrow. I—'

The door was opened by Mrs Peters – the daily woman, who had come to help with the refreshments – spruced up for the occasion in a dress of purple silk with an osprey in her hair.

'Come on in,' she said shortly. 'You'll find 'em al

somewhere or other. I'm in the middle of a lobster salad. I can't stop to see to you now.'

And with a flounce of the purple dress she vanished towards the kitchen.

The man propelled William across the hall and in the first open doorway.

Mr Brown was alone in the room. He had retreated from the party for a few moments' respite. He still felt – secretly, ashamedly – a little aggrieved. This noisy young people's party was not the celebration he would have chosen. He still felt the wistful longing for a peaceful evening with an old crony . . .

He looked coldly at William, then, with a sudden opening of mouth and eyes, at the man who followed him. Incredulity, amazement, delight chased each other over his countenance.

'Well, by everything that's wonderful – old Sandy!' he said.

The man's face showed all the emotions that had chased each other over Mr Brown's.

'Great Scott!' he said. 'If it isn't old Podger!'

'Come along and sit down,' said Mr Brown, drawing up an arm-chair to the fire, his face beaming with pleasure. 'Well, well, well! How many years is it since we met? Are you living in the neighbourhood? When did you come?'

The two began to talk, forgetful of everything and everyone around them. 'Do you remember . . . ?' 'Do you remember . . . ?' ran like a refrain through their conversation.

William stood watching them while the meaning of the strange situation slowly filtered through to his bemused mind. They were old school friends. They hadn't met for years. They were delighted to see each other again.

Silently he tiptoed from the room, replaced Edgar in his box in the garage, then, feeling the need of sustenance, fed himself and Jumble lavishly at the buffet table in the dining-room till discovered and removed by Ethel.

'You've eaten enough to feed a whole zoo,' she said indignantly. 'And I should think it's well past your bedtime.'

It *was* well past William's bedtime. He realised that discretion called for a speedy withdrawal from the festive scene and a pretence of deep sleep in the event of a visit from his father. But the room where his father sat with 'Sandy' held an irresistible fascination for him. Cautiously, warily, he re-entered it. Dancing was going on in the room now, but Mr Brown and his friend, ensconced in their arm-chairs by the fire, seemed unaware of it. They were happy and content on an island of shared memories amid the raging sea of the dancers. Gone was the slightly hang-dog air that Mr Brown had worn earlier in the evening. His face shone with happiness. The impossible had happened. He was spending the evening by his fireside with an old crony . . .

Mrs Brown watched her husband, as happy as he at the turn events had taken.

'He's an old friend of your husband's, isn't he, Mrs Brown?' said Dorita Merton. 'They seem to be enjoying their talk.'

'Yes,' said Mrs Brown, 'and we owe it all to William.' She looked down at William who was standing near her. William stared glassily in front of him, his face wooden and expressionless. 'You see, his father had said that the best present he could give him was a human civilised action and so William managed to find – I don't know how he did it – this old friend who's just come to the neighbourhood and brought him along to the party. It was his present, you see, and quite the best my husband's had. Robert and Ethel had said that William could only have one guest and he brought this guest for his father instead of bringing one for himself. It was such a kind and considerate action.'

The words reached 'Sandy' across the room.

He looked at William and slowly dropped one eyelid.

# Chapter 8

# William and the National Health Service

William and Ginger walked slowly down the road and stopped outside the gate of a largish detached house surrounded by a pleasant wooded garden. At the end of the lawn near the hedge grew a tall chestnut tree with regular symmetrical branches rising to a tapering point. William's eyes were fixed on the tree, Ginger's on the back of the square red brick house that stood at the further end of the lawn.

'They've moved in, you see,' said Ginger. 'They've got curtains up an' everything.'

William had been confined to bed for a week with an attack of 'flu and now, returning to normal life, was outraged to find the empty house, whose garden he and Ginger had appropriated to their own use, occupied by strangers.

'Gosh, it's not fair,' he said indignantly, turning his eyes from the tree to the now trim lawn and neatly curtained windows. 'They've no *right*!'

'They've bought it,' said Ginger mildly. 'When people buy a thing it's theirs. That's the lor, anyway.'

'Well, it's *rotten*,' said William. 'Gosh! All the time I was in bed I was thinkin' about it.'

'I told you someone had bought it.'

'Yes, but I didn't know they were goin' to sneak into it like this while I was in bed. It's a jolly mean trick.'

'You couldn't have stopped them even if you'd been up.'

'Huh!' said William in a voice that implied dark and sinister powers.

'What would you've done to stop 'em when they'd bought it by lor?' challenged Ginger.

'Well, never mind that,' said William evasively. 'What are they like, anyway?'

'Dunno. They're a man an' a woman an' they're called Birtley. They were in the front garden with Archie when I came along to fetch you.'

'Archie?' said William in surprise.

'Oh, yes, I forgot to tell you that,' said Ginger. 'Archie put an advertisement in the local paper saying he'd paint pictures of people's houses for them at a reas'nable price an' this was the only answer he got. I s'pose they were the only ones that didn't know what Archie's paintings are like.'

'Let's go round to the front an' see if they're still there,' said William.

'I dunno that we'd better,' said Ginger uncertainly.

William's insatiable interest in his fellow creatures had, on more than one occasion, landed them in difficulties.

'I only want to have a look at 'em an' see what they're like,' explained William.

'A' right,' agreed Ginger doubtfully.

The Laurels was at the juncture of two roads. William and Ginger skirted the hedge till they came to the front of the house, then hovered in the shelter of the gateway watching the scene that was taking place on the drive.

Archie, looking even more harassed than usual, stood before an easel, with a palette in one hand and a paint brush in the other. On one side of him stood a bristly little man with a face like a Yorkshire terrier's and, on the other, a stout woman with large pendulous cheeks and a small tight mouth. She was inspecting the unfinished painting of the house with a look of grim disapproval.

'I don't like it,' she said.

Archie blinked at her.

'But I haven't finished it,' he expostulated. 'You can't judge it before it's finished.'

'Yes, I can,' said the woman.

'I've only done half of it.'

'Well, I don't like the half you've done.'

'If you can suggest any improvement . . .' said Archie with dignity.

'I'd like a bay window.'

Archie threw a startled glance at the house.

'There isn't a bay window,' he said.

'Well, there's nothing to stop you putting one in, is there?' said the woman tartly. 'I'm paying for the paint, aren't I?'

Archie struggled for a moment in silence with his artistic conscience. The struggle was a short one and the issue never for a moment in doubt. This was the first commission that Archie had ever received in the whole course of his professional career.

'I'll put in a bay window, of course, if you wish,' he said distantly.

The small tight mouth tightened still further.

'What sort of one? I don't want anything cheap-looking.'

'Well – er—' said Archie, baffled. 'I – er – don't quite know. I don't pretend to be an expert on the subject of bay windows.'

'Now listen,' said Mrs Birtley. 'I went to tea with some people at Upper Marleigh yesterday – The Poplars the house was called – and they'd got a real posh slap-up bay window. Built right out into the garden, not just stuck on same as a greenhouse like some of 'em, wasn't it, Wilfred?'

'Certainly, certainly, certainly,' barked the Yorkshire terrier.

Again she looked with disfavour at Archie's painting.

'No, I don't like it. You haven't put any character or old-world charm in it, and the house agent's paper said most particular that it had got character and old-world charm.'

Archie brought an envelope and a pencil out of his pocket.

'If you'll describe this particular bay window,' he said in as icy a tone as he could command.

'You'd only make a mess of it if I did,' snapped the woman. 'The best thing for you to do is to go and have a look at it. It's next door to Boulters Farm.'

'Come on,' said William, drawing Ginger away.

'I didn't see anythin' wrong with it,' said Ginger, as they walked down the road. 'It looked like a house, anyway, an' most of Archie's paintings don't look like anything at all.'

But William was not interested in Archie's painting. He was only interested in the new occupants of The Laurels.

'Gosh, weren't they awful!' he said.

'Yes, we'd better keep clear of 'em,' agreed Ginger.

'Not much use askin' them to let us play in the wood part of their garden.'

They had reached the road that led past the back of the house. William stopped and looked again at the chestnut tree.

'I *said* you couldn't get to the top,' said Ginger with a note of satisfaction in his voice.'

'I nearly did the last time I tried,' said William, 'an' I jolly well *will* the next.'

'There isn't goin' to be a next,' said Ginger.

'Yes, there is,' said William. His face was set in lines of grim determination. 'An' I'll jolly well *show* you.'

'Gosh!' said Ginger in dismay. 'You can't do it now, William. They'd murder you as soon as look at you. I shouldn't be s'prised if they're murderin' poor ole Archie. You'd be takin' your life in your hands an' goin' into the jaws of death.'

'Well, I've often been there an' come out again,' said William. 'I'll be all right. They're both at the front with Archie an' I bet they'll be there for hours talkin' about bay windows an' old-world greenhouses an' things. I'm goin' to have another shot at it, anyway, an' I *bet* I get to the top this time.'

Ginger watched helplessly as William made his way through the hedge and began his assault on the tree. His previous efforts had made him familiar with the lower branches and his progress was rapid. Then, slowly, carefully, he climbed the higher branches till his head emerged at the top. He was on the point of giving vent to a yell of triumph when he noticed that Ginger, in the road below, was making frantic signs to him, waving his arms and pointing to the house.

William peered through the branches. Mr Birtley had just come out of a side door, carrying a deck chair. He carried it across the lawn, set it up at the foot of the chestnut tree, took a newspaper out of his pocket, leant back with an air of relaxation and began to read.

Ginger's signs had become yet more frantic. He was dancing about in the road, pointing up and down the tree and in all directions. William considered his tactics. He couldn't stay where he was much longer. His foothold at the top was precarious and a short broken branch was digging into his stomach. He waited for a few minutes, gazing down at his unconscious host. The hands that held the newspaper dropped . . . the grizzled head dropped . . . there came the sound of deep rhythmic snores: Mr Birtley was asleep. William decided on action. He would descend silently and cautiously on the side of the tree away from Mr Birtley, then creep through the hedge to the road.

Silently and cautiously he began the descent. The only difficult part was a spot half-way down the tree, where a large gap between the branches made it necessary to make use of a foothold on the other side. Clasping the trunk with his arms, he edged himself round, found the foothold, lost it, struggled wildly to regain it, then fell, crashing through the branches on to the sleeping form of Mr Birtley. William, the now fully awakened Mr Birtley and the wreckage of the deck chair rolled together on the ground for a few seconds, then William and Mr Birtley sprang to their feet.

Nimbly, breathlessly, William dodged among the trees. A little less nimbly, a little more breathlessly, Mr Birtley followed. Mr Birtley's Yorkshire terrier face bristled with anger. He uttered short sharp barks of rage as he ran. At one moment his outstretched hand caught William by the neck, but William, neatly disengaging himself, plunged through the hedge and joined Ginger in a headlong flight down the road.

'Gosh!' said William when at last they paused and, looking back apprehensively, found themselves unpursued. 'Gosh! He nearly got me once.'

'I told you you were goin' into the jaws of death,' said Ginger.

'Well, I got out of 'em,' said William airily, 'an' I got to the top of that tree, too. An' we needn't worry about him, 'cause he doesn't know who we are so he can't tell our fathers. Anyway, it was jolly excitin' an' I'm beginning to feel jolly hungry. I bet it's lunch time. What shall we do this afternoon?'

He had dismissed the morning from his mind. The afternoon, full of glorious possibilities, stretched before him.

'I've got to go an' help my aunt clearing out for removing,' said Ginger. 'She's goin' to give me two an' six for it, so it's not too bad an' it won't take long.'

'Yes, an' I've jus' remembered,' said William. 'I've got to go into Hadley for my mother to take somethin' to the cleaners'. I'll come round an' call for you at your aunt's soon as I've done it.'

WILLIAM LOST HIS FOOTHOLD AND FELL, CRASHING THROUGH
THE BRANCHES ON TO MR BIRTLEY.

After lunch William set off for Hadley. He deposited his parcel safely at the cleaners', then walked back towards the bus stop, gazing idly into the shop windows. A model launch in a toy shop attracted his notice. He was looking at it intently when suddenly he heard, as it seemed, a short sharp bark and, turning, saw Mr Birtley, his face distorted by rage, bearing down on him through the crowd. Without a moment's hesitation, William set off at a run. Mr Birtley, too, set off at a run, dodging after William in hot pursuit.

'That's the boy!' he barked as he ran. 'That's the boy!'

They threaded their way through the passers-by. The passers-by watched them, transfixed by amazement.

'Stop him!' barked Mr Birtley.

The passers-by showed signs of recovering from their paralysis. An old lady in a lobster-coloured plush coat made an ineffectual grab at William as he went by. Desperately he plunged into a side street . . . into another side street . . . in at a pair of wide-open gates . . . across a courtyard and through an open doorway. He found himself in a large institutional-looking hall. A queue of people stood before a sort of hatch marked 'Enquiries.' A man lay on an ambulance stretcher by the wall. Another man hobbled towards the door on crutches with a bandaged foot.

William realised that he had made his way into Hadley hospital. No one took any notice of him. He hovered for a few moments by the door, then peeped out. Mr Birtley stood at the gate, throwing quick suspicious glances round the courtyard. Hastily William darted back, colliding with a woman who carried a large shopping basket of groceries.

'Look where you're going, can't you?' she said, putting the basket on to the floor and stooping to pick up a jar of pickles. 'I've just 'ad me feet done an' you've got to go tramplin' on 'em.'

'Sorry,' said William.

He looked out again.

Slowly, resolutely, Mr Birtley was making his way across he courtyard. It was clear that he had seen William enter the gates and was determined not to abandon the chase till he had run his quarry to earth.

'Gosh!' said William despairingly. 'He's turned into a bloodhound now.'

Looking round for further refuge, he tripped over the shopping basket, scrambled to his feet and darted into a room that opened from the entrance hall. It was a long narrow room with chairs ranged on both sides. Most of the chairs were occupied but half-way down the room there was a vacant chair between two large women. Gratefully William slipped into it. After a few moments he peeped out between his two bulwarks. Through the open doorway he could see Mr Birtley hovering in the entrance of the hall. He was evidently a man who did not readily abandon any task that he had set himself. William withdrew again behind his bulky ramparts.

'Wonderful thing, this health service,' one of them remarked to the other over his head. She had a flat placid good-natured face with a slight squint. 'Least thing that goes wrong with you you can come along and get it put right. Takes a load off your mind. A boon to sufferers, it is. Hardly a week goes by,' she added proudly, 'that I don't come along and get somethin' put right. After all, you're payin' for it so you might as well get value for it. No good lettin' the nation's money run to waste.' She held out her hand showing a bandaged finger. 'Broke me finger last week, fallin' off a step-ladder. Got it fixed up here in no time – X-ray an' all. Wonderful things, those X-rays. I've felt a new woman since I had 'em. Put new life into me, they did.' She gazed with interest at the other woman's arm, encased in plaster of Paris and resting on a sling. 'What happened to you?'

'Broke it,' said the other woman. Her flabby double chin wobbled gloomily over a purple knitted scarf. 'Jus' my luck It couldn't have happened to anyone but me. And,' darkly, ' don't think much of this 'ere health service. A racket, that's what it is.'

'Oh, I dunno,' said her neighbour.

'A racket,' persisted the other. 'Well, someone must be makin' somethin' out of it – stands to reason – an' it's not me Who is it, then? That's what I want to know.'

William's eyes were wandering round the room. A woman in a white overall was evidently in charge of it. She held a sheet of paper in her hand and every now and then would call out a name, at which one of the patients would rise and go out of a further door. William threw an anxious glance towards the entrance hall, wondering if the coast was clear. A trapped feeling was coming over him. Probably, even if the coast was clear, he couldn't get up and make good his retreat without attracting the attention of the keen-eyed woman in the white overall. Suddenly he realised that both his neighbours were gazing down at him. The woman with the squint was bending down examining his feet and legs and arms.

'Don't often see anyone at this fracture clinic without splints or plaster,' she said. 'What's your trouble, young 'un? Somethin' internal?'

'Yes,' agreed William hastily. 'Yes, that's what it is. It's somethin' awfully internal.'

'I 'ad a cousin once that broke four ribs,' she said with gloomy relish.

'I've broke all mine,' said William, anxious to establish his right to this temporary refuge. 'Every single one of them.'

'A martyr to bad luck, same as me,' said the woman with the double chin.

'You don't look as if you were in pain,' said the other.

'You can't tell from my face when I'm in pain,' said

William. 'I look jus' the same when I'm in pain an' when I'm not in pain. It's the way my face is made. It can't change.'

'Courage, that's what you've got,' said the woman with the squint. 'Courage an' spirit. A lesson to us all.' She inspected him with deepening interest. 'But it mus' give you a stab of agony sometimes. There mus' be times when you can't hide it.'

'Oh, yes,' said William, ready to sustain his rôle. He contorted his face into an expression of blood-curdling ferocity. 'It gave me one jus' then.'

'One of them broken ribs diggin' into your stomach, likely.'

'All of 'em diggin' into it in diff'rent places,' said William, repeating the grimace. He was beginning to enjoy himself. 'An' into my lungs, too. There's one broke right off that's got into my lungs. It's worked its way there through my blood vessels.'

'Mrs Porter,' called the woman in the white overall.

Still looking back at William in fascinated horror, the woman got up and went through the further door.

'How did you do it?' said his remaining neighbour, fixing her eyes on him avidly. 'Go on. Tell us about it, ducks.'

'I – I fell from a great height,' said William after a moment's reflection.

'What height?' she said.

The credulity of his audience urged him to wilder flights of fancy. He toyed for a moment with the idea of being a paratrooper, then dismissed it.

'A roof,' he said. 'The roof of a burning house.'

'I once heard of a fireman doin' that,' she said, 'an' there wasn't a whole bone left in his body.'

'There isn't in mine,' said William, who now felt a sort of jealousy for his imaginary exploit and wasn't going to have it outshone even by a fireman. So completely was he carried away on the wings of his imagination that he saw the scene quite clearly – the leaping flames, the crashing masonry, the final desperate jump on to the pavement below. 'All over the place, my bones are. There isn't a single one that—'

The woman in the white overall called another name and, slowly, reluctantly, William's audience rose to its feet and went through the further door.

William looked uneasily around. The crowd in the room had thinned. There was only a handful of people left. He took up a woman's magazine from a chair near him and, bending his head over it, pretended to be deeply absorbed in an article on 'Do Careers Women Make Good Wives?' Furtively he glanced up. A thrill of horror ran through him as he saw his pursuer's bristly little face in the doorway.

'James Green,' called the woman in the white overall.

The remnants of the fracture clinic – four women and an old man – looked round at each other. No one moved.

'Don't seem to be here,' said the old man.

'He's a schoolboy, that's all I know about him,' said the woman in the white overall petulantly. 'I'm not really supposed to be on duty here. I'm supposed to be in the physiotherapy department, but half the staff are down with 'flu and we're all at sixes and sevens . . . '

'Well, he don't seem to be here,' said the old man again. 'These young people of today are all the same. No sense of responsibility.'

'Unreliable,' said the woman in a patchy fur beret. 'Wool-gathering. In at one ear and out of the other.'

'No sense of duty,' said the old man.

'No respect,' said the woman in the fur beret.

'James Green!' said the woman in the white overall again.

Mr Birtley was still there. Obviously he was on the point of entering the room in a final effort to run his prey to earth.

Keeping his face turned away from the door, William rose to his feet.

'Why can't you listen!' snapped the woman in the white overall. 'I've called your name twice.'

'Sorry,' muttered William.

He plunged through the further door into a corridor. Someone opened a door on the other side of it, announced 'James Green' and propelled him through it. A man with a luxuriant moustache, a beaked nose and a high domed forehead sat at a small table beneath a window. Two women in white overalls sat at a desk near him behind a pile of files and papers.

'James Green,' read the man from a case-sheet. 'Fracture of the femur . . . ' He raised his eyes from the paper to William's leg. 'Good Lord! Where's the plaster?'

'It came off,' said William desperately.

The three were gazing at him, speechless with amazement.

'No, it didn't come off,' said William, plunging on wildly. 'It got all right, so I took it off. My leg got all right, I mean. I mean, I got hold of a sort of secret cure that cured it. A sort of rare Eastern herb given me by an Indian Yo-yo an' I tried it on my leg an' it cured it so I took off this plaster an' . . . '

His voice trailed away. Though still speechless, his listeners were obviously labouring under some strong emotion and it was clear that in a moment the storm would break.

He rose to his feet with a fixed and glassy smile.

'Well, thank you very much,' he said. 'P'raps I'd better be goin' now . . . '

'This is outrageous!' exploded the doctor.

The door opened and a thin lank boy, his leg encased in plaster of Paris, entered the room, followed by the waiting-room attendant.

'I don't know what's happened,' she said helplessly. 'This boy says he's James Green. He was waiting in the wrong place. He—'

In a flash, William was out of the door, down the corridor,

**IN A FLASH WILLIAM WAS OUT OF THE DOOR.**

across the courtyard and in the street. There were no signs of
Mr Birtley. He had evidently abandoned the chase. William
plunged down the street into the main road and, still running,
reached the bus stop. The bus was on the point of starting. He
flung himself on to it and made his way home.

Mrs Brown came out of the kitchen as he entered the hall.

'Oh, there you are, dear. Did you leave the parcel at the
cleaners'?'

'Oh, yes,' said William. 'I left it at the cleaners' all right.'

'You've been a long time. I suppose you've been having a look round Hadley.'

'Yes,' agreed William. 'I've been havin' a good look round Hadley. I'm goin' to Ginger's aunt's now. He's helpin' her get ready to remove. I thought I'd jus' call for Jumble an' take him along with me.'

'Oh, yes, poor Jumble! He must have caught his leg on a thorn or something. It's not much of a scratch. He's limping a bit but I think he's putting it on.'

Hearing William's voice, Jumble came rollicking in at the door. He leapt exuberantly at William, then, remembering the gratifying interest his limp had caused earlier in the morning, began to limp round the room, a complacent expression on his long foolish face.

'It ought to be in plaster of Paris,' said William, adopting a professional air and frowning down at Jumble. 'He's prob'ly fractured his femur.'

'Nonsense, dear! He's not fractured anything. A walk will do him good.'

Jumble seemed to agree and the two set off, Jumble frisking about as usual except when, occasionally, he remembered his limp and turned melancholy soulful eyes on William to make sure that he was watching.

Ginger was at the door of his aunt's house when William reached it.

'I've been helpin' her clear out cupboards an' things,' he said. 'It's all finished now, an' she's given me the half-crown so—'

'One moment, boys!' called Ginger's aunt from upstairs.

They clattered up the wooden uncarpeted staircase, enjoying the sound of their heavy shoes, stamping on each step to extract the utmost enjoyment from it.

Ginger's aunt – a brisk, pleasant-looking woman – stood at the top of the stairs, holding a cardboard hat-box.

'We cleared out the medicine cupboard, you remember, dear,' she said to Ginger, 'and packed the things in here, but I've decided not to keep them, after all . . . I've had most of them for years and I expect they've lost any goodness they had by now, so I think I'll start from scratch, as it were, in the new house and just buy new medicines as I need them. So will you two boys take them and tip them into the dust-bin as you go out?'

Ginger took the box and the two clattered downstairs again.

'Here's the dust-bin,' said Ginger, opening the door that led into the backyard.

A thoughtful look had come into William's face.

'Wait a minute!' he said. 'I've got an idea.'

'What is it?'

'Well, listen,' said William earnestly. 'This health service . . . It's a smashing idea, this health service, an' I don't see why animals shouldn't have it, same as yumans. Look at poor ole Jumble. He's got a bad foot an' nowhere for him to go to get it put right.'

'He doesn't look as if he had a bad foot,' said Ginger, watching Jumble, who was chasing a dead leaf round the garden.

'That's his courage an' his spirit,' said William. 'He's a lesson to us all. Anyway, I don't think it's right for yumans to have this health service an' not animals. There isn't any *justice* in it.'

'There's vets,' said Ginger.

'Yes, but you've got to pay vets. This other thing's free.'

'No, it's not. You pay a bit each week.'

'Well, animals could pay a bit each week. I don't see why they shouldn't have this load taken off their mind, same as yumans.'

'Well, there isn't one for animals, so we can't do anythin' about it.'

'Yes, we can. We can start one. Look at all the things in this box.' He turned over the bottles and cartons, reading their labels. 'There's stuff for indigestion an' coughs an' sore throats an' – an' brittle nails an' open pores. There's somethin' for everythin' that could poss'bly go wrong with them. Gosh, Ginger! We could start one straight away.'

'I bet no one'd come to it.'

'I bet they would. They'd have to pay a penny a week, of course.'

'Well, I bet they wouldn't do *that*.'

'P'raps not,' said William, reluctantly facing reality, 'but they might pay a bullseye or a lollypop or somethin'. It'd be better than nothin'.'

'I bet they wouldn't.'

'I bet they would.' He turned to look at the box again. 'We've got a smashin' lot of stuff. Let's try somethin' out on Jumble. Hi, Jumble!'

He caught the reluctant Jumble, found the small harmless-looking scratch on his leg and held his struggling form with difficulty.

'Find somethin' for it, quick, Ginger.'

Ginger rummaged in the box.

'Here's somethin' for heartburn,' he said.

William, tightening his hold on Jumble, placed a hand on his backbone.

'No, I can't feel his heart burnin',' he said. 'Find somethin' else.'

'Here's somethin' called "embrocation",' said Ginger, reading the label on the bottle. 'It says it's good for sprains an' – an' spavin' an'—'

'I 'spect spavin's what he's got,' said William. Jumble's struggles were growing uncontrollable. 'Shove some on quick.'

Ginger uncorked the bottle and dabbed the white liquid on

Jumble's leg. Jumble freed himself with a final effort and,
light-headed with relief, raced madly round the garden.

'There! It's cured him,' said William. 'I knew it
would . . . Now let's get the thing started. Let's go'n' write
out the notice an' fetch Henry an' Douglas.'

They carried the box to Ginger's house, wrote the notice in
Ginger's bedroom, then went to the old barn to fix the notice
on the door.


Annymals nashonal helth servis.

annymals kured of all deceases starting too oklock
tomorro fre ecsept for peny a week bulseys and loly-
pops kan be givven insted William Brown will make a
speach.

cined William Brown.


'There!' said William as he secured the notice to the door
with a rusty nail, using the heel of his shoe as a hammer. 'I
*bet* they'll all come.'


At two o'clock the next afternoon William, Ginger, Henry,
Douglas and Jumble had taken up their positions in the old
barn.

'I bet it'll get into even more of a muddle than that old Pets'
Club did,' said Douglas gloomily, 'if anyone comes, that is,
an' I bet they won't.'

But already patients and their escorts were arriving. Frankie
Miller came first, carrying a cat; Ella Poppleham followed with
a Pekinese; Freddy Parker brought a canary in a cage; Victor
Jameson a lizard in a box and Jimmy Barlow a dejected-looking hen under his arm. William noted with relief that Arabella
Simpkin (who had a gift for trouble-making which she had
brought to a fine art) was not among them. Odds and ends of

children straggled in, carrying a varied selection of dogs, cats, birds and insects. An animated hubbub arose – barks, mews, growls and high-pitched children's voices.

'Go on, William! Tell us about it!'

William had dragged forward the packing-case that was the sole furniture of the old barn and mounted it carefully.

'Ladies an' gentlemen an' animals,' he began, 'an' shut up, everyone. I'm goin' to make this speech.' The uproar continued unabated. 'Shut *up*, everyone! I can't hear myself speak.'

'Well, you're not missing much,' said Maisie Fellowes.

William ignored the interruption.

'Shut *up*!' he said again, raising his voice to a raucous bellow.

The uproar died away.

William cleared his throat with an air of self-importance.

'I'll start all over again, 'case you didn't hear me the first time.' He cleared his throat again. 'Lades an' gentlemen an' animals, I'm goin' to tell you about this animals' national health service we've started. It takes this load off these animals' minds an' it's a boon to sufferers. You've got to pay a penny a week for it.' A rising murmur of protest interrupted him. 'Well, anyway a lollypop or a bulls-eye or somethin', an' we'll cure your animals of all their diseases. Now listen' – he raised his voice to quell the renewed uproar – 'I'll show you a cure I've done on Jumble. Jumble hurt his foot yesterday, so's he couldn't walk without limpin' an' I cured him with medicine out of this box.' He got down from the packing-case and lifted the hat-box on to it. 'Today he's running about as if he'd never hurt his foot at all.' He looked round. 'Hi, Jumble!'

Ginger dragged Jumble from a game of catch-as-catch-can with the Pekinese and put him at William's feet.

'There he is!' said William, pointing to him dramatically. '*Cured!*'

Jumble, finding all eyes turned on him, decided to repeat the trick that had originally won him his position as centre of attention. Slowly and as if painfully, he limped across the barn. William was disconcerted, but only for a moment.

'He's tryin' to show you what he was like before he was cured,' he said. 'It's jolly intelligent of him. He'll start showin' you he's cured soon.'

William's prophecy was fulfilled, for Jumble, in his slow laborious progress, suddenly met the Peke again, and the game of catch-as-catch-can was resumed with increased vigour.

'There!' said William triumphantly. 'I told you, didn't I? Now make a queue an' come up an' bring your animals to be cured.'

Frankie Miller came first with his cat – an ancient, somnolent tortoiseshell with rusty fur.

'What's wrong with it?' said William.

Frankie considered.

'It's got a funny mew,' he said at last.

'What d'you mean, a funny mew?' said William.

'Well, it mews like this,' said Frankie, emitting a deep husky roar, ''stead of like this same as other cats.' He gave a shrill squeak.

'Got a sore throat,' said William. He turned to his assistants. 'Find somethin' for a sore throat.'

'Here's somethin',' said Henry, bringing a bottle out of the box. 'It says "Throat Paint" an' there's a little brush tied on to it.'

'That'll do,' said William.

He parted the fur on the cat's neck, plunged the paintbrush in to the bottle and dabbed it on. The cat gave a shrill cry of protest.

'Gosh, that's a better mew,' said Frankie. 'It's cured all right.'

'Next!' said William.

'It's a lizard,' said Victor Jameson, opening his box.

'What's wrong with it?' said William.

'Well, it sleeps nearly all the time an' – an' it's got a funny sort of look on its face.'

It was clear that the animal-owners had come more in a spirit of curiosity than because their pets were suffering from any specific diseases.

'Here's a face lotion,' said Ginger, dragging a bottle out of the box and reading the label. 'It says it imparts new life to the complexion.'

'That'll do,' said William.

The lizard opened its eyes and gave William a reproachful look as he anointed it generously from the bottle.

'Yes, it looks a bit diff'rent now,' admitted Victor as he gazed down at his pet, thickly coated with the preparation of a famous beauty expert.

'Wash it off before it goes to bed,' said William. 'Next!'

A three-year-old pushed his way to the front, holding up a scratched finger.

'Make it better,' he demanded.

'Gosh, no!' You're a yuman,' said William indignantly. 'I don't do yumans.'

The small face crumpled up into tears.

'Want it made better,' he wailed.

'Oh, all right,' said William, seizing the nearest bottle and pouring liquid 'Toothache Cure' over the outstretched finger.

The chubby face broke into a beaming smile.

'Better now,' he said as he trotted happily away.

Then Arabella Simpkin appeared. She carried a basket and there was a look of malicious triumph on her face. She approached William and held out the basket.

'It's a hedgehog,' she said, 'an' it's got backache. You'll have to rub something in.'

'IT'S GOT BACKACHE,' SAID ARABELLA SIMPKIN.
'YOU'LL HAVE TO RUB SOMETHING IN.'

It was clear that Arabella had given much thought and ca
to the preparation of her patient.

But the time for detailed diagnosis was past. The crow
was milling round William, demanding instant treatment f
their pets. William took hold of a bottle of eye lotion ar
sprinkled it lavishly over the hedgehog's spikes.

'You've got to rub it in,' said Arabella.

'No, that sort of backache cure's got to soak in,' sa
William. 'It won't do any good unless it *soaks* in.'

'Oh,' said Arabella, accepting defeat and walking quiet
away.

William continued to treat his patients. He gave castor c

to a dormouse, a mild sleeping draught to the hen, a cough lozenge to a Corgi and a puff of deodorant to the canary in the cage.

Then a diversion was caused by the entrance of Caroline Jones, leading a young pig by her skipping rope.

'It doesn't belong to me,' she said, 'but I haven't got an animal an' I wanted to come an' I found it in Emstead Lane an' I thought it didn't look well so I brought it along.'

The piglet sat down on its haunches and gazed trustingly at William. The others gathered round discussing its symptoms.

'Looks like heartburn to me,' said Ginger.

'I think it's jus' tired,' said Henry.

'Wants a tonic,' said Douglas.

'Here's some hair tonic,' said Henry, diving into the hat-box.

'That'll do,' said William. 'It'll do its hair good, anyway.'

But the pig had got up and made its way to a small empty carton that had contained a bottle of aspirins. It ate it with every appearance of enjoyment, moved on a few paces, ate a paper bag in which Victor Jameson had brought an ice-cream, moved on further, ate some orange peel and a banana skin, then sat down again on the ground and gazed round, grunting contentedly.

'There!' said William triumphantly. 'It's ate what it needed to cure it. Animals've got *instinct* to tell 'em what they need

to cure 'em, an' this one's instinct told it to eat the things it'
ate to make it well. Looks all right now, doesn't it?'

'It was my orange peel,' said Maisie Fellowes. 'I cured it. I
ought to pay me something.'

William was raising a spirited objection to this when a red
haired boy with a goldfish in a bowl pushed his way to th
front.

'Make it well,' he shouted. 'Do something to it.'

'What's wrong with it?' said William.

'You're supposed to know that,' countered the boy
'Thought you were an animal doctor.'

'Well—' William was beginning in a noncommittal voice
when Henry, who had been making a further examination of
the contents of the box, interrupted him.

'Gosh, here's a bag full of bandages. Heaps of 'em. We've
not used any bandages.'

'Let's bandage it,' said William, surrendering to a sudde
spirit of irresponsibililty. 'Let's bandage the goldfish.'

'It'll die out of water,' protested Victor Jameson.

'Not if we're quick,' said William.

He inserted his finger into the bowl, brought out the gold
fish, twisted round it the bandage that Henry handed to him
and replaced it. Exhilarated, apparently, by its experience, th
goldfish began to swim nimbly round and round the bow
The bandage detached itself and sank to the bottom.

'It's come off!' shouted its owner indignantly.

'It'll do it jus' as much good in the water with it,' William
assured him. 'It's a jolly good thing for a goldfish, havin'
bandage in the water with it. Didn't you know that?'

'Yes, 'course I did,' said the goldfish owner, who neve
liked to appear at a loss. 'I'd jus' forgot.'

But the spirit of irresponsibility was spreading over th
whole gathering. Animal owners crowded round William
thrusting their pets at him.

'Bandage it!' they shouted. 'Bandage it!'

Bandages were unrolled, tied round the patients and secured by large tight knots. The small boy who had demanded a remedy for his scratched finger now brought a sugar mouse from his pocket and shrilly demanded a bandage. Bandages became entangled with each other. Patients became entangled with each other. The Peke and the Corgi had been bandaged with different ends of the same bandage and were fighting it out, in well-matched and apparently deadly combat. The clinic had become a pandemonium of distracted patients, tearing off their own and each other's bandages. Suddenly the Peke and the Corgi, having evidently come to some sort of working agreement, ran out of the open door and across the field, side by side, linked by a thin white strip. The owners set off in pursuit.

Unable to resist the lure of the chase, the rest of the children followed, animals at their heels or in their arms, bandages flying like pennons in the breeze. William, Ginger, Henry and Douglas were left alone in the barn with the pig.

'Hi! *Caroline!*' shouted William from the door.

Caroline stopped for a moment in her headlong flight.

'You've left your pig behind,' said William.

'I don't want it,' said Caroline. 'It's not mine, anyway. I found it in Emstead Lane. You can keep it,' and turned to fly across the field in the wake of the crowd of children and the fluttering bandages.

The four boys stood examining the pig. It was sitting on its haunches again, looking at them with small bright trusting eyes.

'Wonder where it came from,' said William.

'Might be one of old Jenks' pigs,' said Ginger.

'I'll go 'n' see,' said Henry, who possessed a certain rudimentary sense of law and order. 'We must take it back if it is.'

He set out across the field to Jenks' farm.

'Well, it went off all right,' said Ginger a little doubtfully.

'It went off jolly well,' said William. 'I cured the whole lo
of 'em. Gosh! There wasn't much wrong with them by the
time I'd finished with them.'

'I don't think there was much wrong with them to star
with,' said Ginger.

'We've not made much out of it,' said Douglas, surveying
the half-sucked lollypop and the bulls-eye, thickly coated
with pocket fluff, that were the sole contributions of the
attendants at the clinic.

The pig, as if to remind them of its presence, gave a half
grunt, half-squeak.

'It's hungry again,' said William. 'Let's get it something to
eat.'

Going into the field they collected grass, leaves and, from
beneath an oak tree that grew from the hedge, as many acorns
as their pockets would hold. The pig ate them eagerly.

It was while Douglas was offering it the half-sucked lolly
pop that Henry entered breathlessly.

'No, it's not one of ole Jenks',' he said. 'Old Jenks wasn'
in but his wife was an' she counted them an' they were al
there an' she said it mus' be one of Smith's so I went t
Smith's an' it wasn't one of his an' he said it mus' be one c
Jenks' so it isn't either's.'

They gazed at their guest in perplexity. There seemed to b
a glint of sardonic amusement in the small bright eyes.

'I bet it's a wild pig,' said William at last.

'There aren't any,' said Henry.

'How d'you know there aren't?' said William. 'Gosh! A
animals were wild to start with. There were wild cats an' wil
dogs an' wild sheep an' – an' wild cows all over the place
Most of 'em got tamed with civ'lisation, but I bet they a
didn't. I bet there's been wild families of 'em hidin' up i
woods an' places all these years. I bet this pig belongs to

fam'ly of wild pigs that's been hidin' up somewhere for gen'rations an' it'd jus' come out to look for food when Caroline Jones found it.'

'It doesn't *act* wild,' said Ginger, surveying the placid pink figure before them.

'That doesn't mean it *isn't* wild,' said William. 'Yumans are s'posed to be tamed an' there's hundreds of 'em that act wild. Gosh! I'm always comin' across yumans that act wild. Well, this pig's wild but it acts tame. It's the same thing only the other way round.'

They were obviously impressed by this argument.

'What'll we do with it, then?' said Henry.

'Well, if it's wild it belongs to anyone, same as caterpillars an' insects,' said William. His face glowed with the light of an idea. 'Let's keep it. Gosh! Fancy havin' a real pig all of our own!'

'I bet our mothers won't let us,' said Douglas.

'They needn't know at first,' said William. 'We'll hide it at first, then break it to them gradually bit by bit.'

'An' where'll we hide it?' said Douglas, a note of sarcasm invading his gloom. 'Jus' tell me that. Where'll we *hide* a live pig?'

'Oh, shut up makin' objections,' said William irritably. 'There mus' be hundreds of places to hide a wild pig that acts tame same as this one does . . . Gosh! I've got an idea. There's your garage, Ginger. No one ever goes into it, do they?'

Ginger's family did not possess a car and the garage was stocked with household articles that had been turned out of the house in greater or lesser stages of disrepair. Ginger's mother was a 'hoarder' and never got rid of anything in case it 'came in' later.

'No,' said Ginger. 'That should be all right – if it keeps quiet.'

'I bet it will,' said William.

'What'll we call it?' said Henry. 'It ought to have a name now it's our pet.'

'It looks jus' like my uncle Ernest,' said Douglas. 'He's got eyes and a nose jus' like that.'

'All right, we'll call it Ernest,' said William. 'Come on, Ernest. Let's take him to Ginger's garage.'

They led their new pet, still secured by the skipping rope, across the fields to Ginger's house. Ernest looked at his new surroundings with interest, investigated a broken mincing machine, nosed round a dressmaker's dummy (which Ginger's mother had outgrown) then settled down on an old sack in the corner and composed himself to sleep. Silently the four crept out and fastened the door.

'Well, he seems to like it all right,' said William. 'I b'lieve he was tired of bein' a wild one an' is jolly glad to start bein' a tame one. We'll all come here tomorrow morning an' bring him a bit of breakfast.'

'An' you'd better go now,' said Ginger, glancing nervously towards the house. 'There's goin' to be an awful mess-up if my father finds him.'

'I bet there'll be a mess-up anyway,' said Douglas with a hollow laugh.

Cautiously, anxiously, they opened the garage door the next morning. To their relief Ernest was still there. He ran to them with little squeals of pleasure. They gazed down at him, their hearts swelling with the pride of ownership. Even Jumble seemed to accept him as a friend.

From bulging pockets they brought their contributions to Ernest's breakfast. Henry had brought a paper bag filled with porridge, Douglas half a dozen bacon rinds and some fried bread, William a mixture of sardine and marmalade in an old tobacco tin, Ginger a slab of treacle tart left over from yesterday's lunch. Ernest ate them greedily.

'Well, he's had a jolly good breakfast,' said Ginger.

But William was gazing down at their pet with a worried frown.

'I don't believe we're feedin' him right,' he said.

'It's jolly good food,' said Ginger indignantly. 'I'd have liked to eat that treacle tart myself.'

'Yes, but it's yuman food,' said William. 'It ought to be pig's food.'

'Well, what is pig's food?'

'I dunno, but I'm goin' to find out.'

'How?'

'Well, there's a new farmer called Mr Furnace at Boulters Farm in Upper Marleigh. I've heard people talkin' about him. He does everything in a new sci'ntific way, so he mus' have a new sci'ntific way of feedin' pigs an' I'm goin' over to see what it is.'

'Y-yes,' said Ginger. 'It's not a bad idea.'

'We might get a prize for him if we feed him up properly,' said Henry. 'When are you goin'?'

'Now,' said William, setting off towards the gate. 'An' I'd better not take Jumble or any of you. It might make him mad to have a lot of people messin' about.'

'Well, I'll be s'rprised to see you comin' back alive.' said Douglas.

'Gosh, I'm not afraid of him,' said William.

But something of his courage deserted him as he approached the spreading buildings of Boulters Farm. He hung about the entrance looking at the large barns, the clean-swept yard, the modern hay stacks, the tractor, the mechanical reaper and binder. Presently a man, wearing breeches and leather gaiters, came out of the farm and crossed the yard towards one of the outbuildings. He was large and broad-shouldered, and the lines of his weather-beaten face showed grimness and resolution. He was obviously Mr Furnace

himself, and obviously he was not a man to be trifled with. He
directed a suspicious glance at William before he vanished
into the shed, and the rest of William's courage oozed away.
He decided not to risk a personal interview. Peering through
the gate he saw a line of pigsties at the further end of the
courtyard. He would slip across and see what the pigs were
eating as soon as the coast was clear.

Mr Furnace crossed the courtyard again to the house, throwing another suspicious glance at William. The coast seemed to
be clear, so, keeping in the shelter of the barn, William slipped

across to the pigsties. They were magnificent structures of cement, scrubbed clean inside and out. He peeped over an enclosure, lined with feeding troughs. Several young pigs were running about, and he caught a glimpse of more pigs in the inner sty beyond. Climbing over the low wall, he made his way into the further recesses of the sty. A large sow, lying in a corner, eyed him languidly, and the pigs set up a loud squealing. Hearing footsteps, William craned his neck round the opening and saw Mr Furnace approaching the sty, carrying a bucket in each hand. The farmer opened the gate and poured the contents of the buckets into one of the feeding troughs. A loud squealing arose as the pigs surrounded it. The sow got lumberingly to its feet and went to join them.

WITH A BELLOW OF RAGE MR FURNACE DARTED AFTER
WILLIAM.

Unable to restrain his curiosity, William again craned his neck round the aperture. Unfortunately, at that moment Mr Furnace straightened himself, turned round and – met William's eye. With a bellow of rage he darted towards him. William plunged through the pigs, fell into the trough, picked himself up, scrambled over the wall and, dripping with pig food, fled out of the farmyard and across the field.

He found Henry and Douglas at the gate of Ginger's house.

'Did you find out what they eat?' said Henry.

'Yes,' said William. He looked down at his sodden jacket. 'They eat this, but I don't know what it's made of.'

'Didn't he tell you?'

'No. I didn't ask him . . . Gosh! I seem to've been run after by people ever since I got up yesterday.' An aggrieved note crept into his voice. 'There's days when it seems people jus' can't leave me in peace. Where's Ginger?'

'His mother called him in to help her move the hall chest so's she could clean behind it.'

At that moment Ginger joined them. There was a look of consternation on his face.

'I say! An awful thing's happened,' he said. 'Mrs Monk's jus' telephoned my mother an' she's havin' a jumble sale tomorrow an' she wants some stuff an' my mother said she could come over this afternoon an' look through all that junk in the garage an' – Gosh! What about Ernest?'

The four held a hasty consultation. Douglas's and Henry's garages were occupied by their families' cars. William's garage was, to all intents and purposes, an extension of the kitchen, with store cupboards, firewood, coke and clothes-horse.

'She's in an' out all day,' said William. 'She'd find him in no time if we put him there.'

'It's only jus' for the afternoon,' said Ginger. 'It'll be safe again when she's gone through the stuff.'

'*Tell* you what!' said William. 'I've got an idea.'

'What?'

'Archie's cottage.'

'Archie's cottage?'

'Yes. There's that bedroom – the one he doesn't use – with no furniture in. It'd make a *smashing* pigsty jus' for the afternoon.'

'Wouldn't he mind?' said Douglas.

'He won't know. He's out all day painting that ole house. He won't be back till it's dark an' we'll have got Ernest out of it by then. We needn't bother Archie about it at all. He never locks his doors so we can get in all right. He won't even know we've been, an' I bet he wouldn't mind if he did.'

'It's worth trying,' said Henry judicially.

''Course it is,' said William. 'It's a *smashin*' idea. Ginger an' me'll take him. 'S no good all of us goin'. We don't want people to know about Ernest yet an' people are more likely to notice four boys an' a pig than two boys an' a pig.'

There appeared to be logic in his argument. The other two agreed. Keeping a wary eye on the windows of Ginger's house, they opened the garage door and ushered Ernest, still attached to his skipping rope, down to the gate. Ernest trotted briskly and happily, glad, as it seemed, to escape from the company of the dressmaker's dummy. Henry and Douglas stood at the gate and watched the trio out of sight.

Fate seemed for once to favour William. The road was empty. Unchallenged, they made their way to Archie's cottage, opened the door and led Ernest inside.

'Archie?' called William a little apprehensively.

There was no reply.

'It's all right,' said William. 'He's still out painting. Come on! Let's get Ernest upstairs.'

Ernest tackled the stairs with unexpected agility and uttered little squeals of excitement on entering the bedroom.

'He's jolly intelligent,' said William, gazing fondly down at the round pink form. 'Gosh! He's goin' to be the best pet we've ever had – except Jumble, of course.'

Ginger, who had gone to the window, gave a sudden gasp of dismay.

'*William!*'

'Yes?'

'Here's Archie comin' back.'

'Gosh!'

Standing well away from the window, they watched Archie's thin, harassed-looking figure as it flitted from gate to door.

'What are we goin' to do now?' whispered Ginger.

'Let's wait. He's prob'ly jus' come back for a pencil or indiarubber he forgot. I bet he'll be out again in a minute.'

Archie had gone straight to the telephone and rung a Hadley number.

'Is that you, doctor?' they heard him say. His voice was high-pitched and agitated. 'I'm in a terrible jam and I want you to help me. My nerves are shattered. Simply *shattered* . . . Yes, I'll begin at the beginning. You see' – a note of pride invaded his voice – 'I got a commission to paint The Laurels for Mr and Mrs Birtley, and she wanted a bay window in it . . . No, there isn't a bay window but she wanted one. She wanted one like the bay window at The Poplars over in Upper Marleigh and she sent me there to sketch it. I had to go three times because each time there was something she didn't like about it. Well, as I was coming back in my car from the third visit yesterday afternoon, I had to pass Boulters Farm, you know, and there was a pig outside in the middle of the road and I tried to pass it but it began to run on in front of the car and the more I tried to pass it the faster it ran, making the most *frightful* noise.

'The ghastly business went on till I was nearly home and

then the pig turned into Emstead Lane. I came home and put the car away and then it occurred to me that I ought to do something about it so I went to Emstead Lane but there was no sign of it, and I took for granted that it had found its way home. Animals do, you know. It's a form of instinct. Well, I didn't sleep a wink all night and this morning a dreadful man called Mr Furnace, who evidently owns the farm, came and said he'd got witnesses to prove that I'd driven the pig away and demanding the pig or £50 compensation. I haven't *got* £50, doctor, and I can't find the pig. I've hunted high and low, and my nerves are in such a state that I can hardly hold a paint brush. I want you to give me something to pull me together. Just till I've finished this painting . . . You'll come along? That's awfully good of you. Thank you so much. Good-bye.'

The click of the receiver was followed by a thunderous knocking at the door. Archie opened it. Leaning over the banister, William and Ginger saw the set angry face of Mr Furnace.

'I've come for the fifty pounds,' he said, thrusting his burly form through the door that Archie was ineffectually trying to shut against him.

'I've not *got* fifty pounds,' said Archie desperately.

'Give me back my pig, then.'

'I can't *find* your pig. I keep telling you I can't find your pig.'

At that moment the door burst open again and Mr Birtley entered.

'My wife says she wants yellow curtains at that bay window,' he said breathlessly.

The farmer ignored the interruption.

'I've got three independent witnesses ready to swear on oath in a court of law that they saw you deliberately drive that pig away from my farm and out of the village.'

'I didn't drive it. It went. It kept on going and going and—'

'A deep gold yellow, she says,' said Mr Birtley, thrusting his Yorkshire terrier face between them.

'A Landrace pedigree, that pig is,' said the farmer, still ignoring the newcomer. 'Fifty pounds compensation, you'll have to pay, and costs as well if I bring it to court.'

'I tell you I haven't—'

'And climbing roses,' said Mr Birtley.

'I bought that pig to build up a strain.'

'Pink roses, she says she wants.'

'Daylight robbery.'

'Climbing up the piers and meeting at the top, as it were.'

'Ran over it as like as not and buried the body.'

Archie turned his anguished face from one to the other.

'I didn't . . . I hadn't . . . I never . . . I couldn't . . . ' he said incoherently.

The argument was still going on when a third man arrived – a tall thin man with luxuriant moustaches, a beaked nose and a high domed forehead.

'Oh, doctor!' said Archie. 'I'm so glad you've come.'

'Gosh!' breathed William, drawing back from the banisters.

'How are you feeling now, Mannister?' said the doctor solicitously.

'Worse,' said Archie wildly. 'Much worse.'

Fragments of the conversation continued to float up to the listening couple.

'A pedigree Landrace stole off my farm in broad daylight. I suppose you'll tell me it vanished into thin air.'

'Well, it *did*,' said Archie, his voice sounding like the rising note of an air raid warning.

'Take it easy, Mannister,' came in the deep voice of the doctor.

'And she says the front door looks too ordinary. She wants a porch to it.'

As William had already learnt, Mr Birtley was a man with a one-track mind.

'Relax the tension, Mannister,' counselled the doctor. 'Take a deep breath.'

'You were seen by three independent witnesses who'll swear in a court of law—'

Archie turned on his tormentor with the courage of despair:

'Perhaps you think I've got the creature hidden in the garden in a shed or something.'

'Ease up, Mannister. Loosen your muscles.'

'A porch with pillars.'

'I certainly thought you might have, but I had a good look at your sheds and things as I came in.'

'Then perhaps you think I've got it hidden in the house,' said Archie with a high-pitched sarcastic laugh.

At that moment the unmistakable sound of a grunt came from the room above. A sudden silence fell on the group. The farmer's face turned red, Archie's green.

'Gosh!' whispered William. 'Let's go back to it an' try'n' keep it quiet.'

They crept back into the room. Ernest greeted them with squeals of delight. There came the sound of Mr Furnace's voice saying, 'I'm going to get to the bottom of this,' then the sound of four pairs of feet ascending the staircase.

William and Ginger looked round. The only article of furniture in the room was a sort of hanging wardrobe consisting of a corner cut off by a curtain. They plunged behind it just as the four men entered. Ernest greeted the newcomers with squeals of welcome. Mr Furnace turned a beetroot-coloured face to Archie.

'And *now* what have you got to say for yourself?' he said.

Archie was past saying anything. He could only gibber soundlessly. Mr Furnace made a plunge at Ernest. Ernest neatly evaded capture, squealing loudly, running nimbly

IT WAS WILLIAM ON WHOM THE INTEREST CENTRED.

round the room, diving at last behind the curtained recess and throwing William and Ginger off their balance. They rolled into the room, picked themselves up and then stood gazing sheepishly at the amazed spectators.

But it was William on whom the interest centred.

'*You're* the boy who—' began Mr Birtley, bristling suddenly with rage.

'*You're* the boy who—' roared the farmer.

'*You're* the boy who—' said the doctor.

William looked at the three angry faces thrust close to his. Retribution was inevitable. Best get it over as soon as possible.

'*You're* the boy who—' they bellowed again simultaneously.

'Yes,' said William, surrendering himself to fate. 'Yes, I'm them.'